'In the detailing of lower-middle-class urban life, Jha is nothing short of brilliant. He reminded me of things I had forgotten ... The stories within the narrative (a millworker's obsession with his pigeons, the journey of a rural woman into urban drudgery as a housemaid) are told with conviction and grace'

Jerry Pinto, *Literary Review*

'Mesmerizing. An unnerving, erotic puzzle that works through exquisite and excruciating glimpses. It uncovers a secret intimacy, a haunting mix-up, between violence and love, yearning and beauty and fear ... I admire the way Raj Kamal Jha gets under the skin, behind the eyes, even into the hormones of his characters. And the prose is searingly simple with a beautiful edge of immediacy. It struck me as that rare treat: a truly unusual read'

Andrea Ashworth, author of *Once in a House on Fire*

'He has a talent for affecting and immensely descriptive language, thick with poetry; a keen and observant eye . . . He has an intuitive feeling for the wistful fleeting and sensual nature of memory, and the book is full of intensely evocative and lyrical passages, describing small moments that magnify the fickle nature of time and memory . . . watch out for this exciting new writer'

Sunil Badami, *Sydney Morning Herald*

'Raj Kamal Jha knows how to take us by the scruff of our clichés, lead us down seemingly predictable paths, and then swerve sharply sideways'

Ophelia Field, *Times Literary Supplement*

'An incredibly powerful and original voice. It was like a symphony in words'

Mariella Frostrup

'*The Blue Bedspread* is important because it is authentic in its voice, in its depiction of the internal sensibility of a culture that is enervated, exhausted, driven by pain and despair and joylessness to the very edge. From that edge comes a re-affirmation of strength, a revalidation of joy'

Namita Gokhale, *The Hindu*

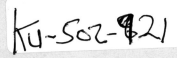
KU-502-921

'Most striking is the spare, sometimes bleak yet tender evocation of Calcutta, this congested "city of twelve million names" through images of rain, flood and snow-fall, and an insistent attention to light. It is this sense of a city, with its undertow of violence redeemed by love and imagination . . . that gives the book its grace'

Maya Jaggi, *Guardian*

'*The Blue Bedspread* is written in a style which is intimate and full of stillness. The story itself is deeply compelling and shocking'

Colm Tóibín

'Jha's writing is fluent and he displays a keen eye for Calcutta life'

Phil Whitaker, *New Statesman*

'If you want to get ahead of the literary game this year, practise getting your jaws around the following syllables: Raj Kamal Jha . . . precise yet bewitching prose'

Peter Popham, *Independent on Sunday*

THE BLUE
BEDSPREAD

Raj Kamal Jha was born in 1966 and spent his first eighteen years in Calcutta. He returned to the city in 1992 as an editor with the *Statesman*. He now lives in New Delhi, where he is an editor on the *Indian Express*. *The Blue Bedspread* won the 1999 Commonwealth Writers Prize for Best First Book (Eurasia).

First published 1999 by Picador

This edition published 2022 by Picador
an imprint of Pan Macmillan,
The Smithson, 6 Briset Street, London EC1M 5NR
EU representative: Macmillan Publishers Ireland Ltd, 1st Floor,
The Liffey Trust Centre, 117–126 Sheriff Street Upper,
Dublin 1, D01 YC43
Associated companies throughout the world
www.panmacmillan.com

ISBN 978-1-0350-0483-6

A CIP catalogue record for this book is available from
the British Library.

1 3 5 7 9 8 6 4 2

Typeset by SetSystems Ltd, Saffron Walden, Essex
Printed and bound by CPI Group (UK) Ltd, Croydon, CR0 4YY

For my father and my mother,
Munishwar and Ranjana Jha

Acknowledgements

I wish to thank:

My agents Gillon Aitken and Emma Parry, for their kindness and their patience.

The team at Picador, including the publisher, Peter Straus, for having the faith; and my editor, Mary Mount, for helping me improve this book.

Pankaj Mishra, for being there.

Shekhar Gupta, Editor-in-Chief, *The Indian Express*, for giving me the space.

Sujata Bose, my first reader and love, my partner in everything.

Sometimes I have to console myself with the fact that he who has lived a lie loves the truth.

– Ingmar Bergman, The Magic Lantern

FIRST STORY

I could begin with my name but forget it, why waste time, it doesn't matter in this city of twelve million names. I could begin with the way I look but what do I say, I am not a young man any more, I wear glasses, my stomach droops over the belt of my trousers.

There's something wrong with my trousers. The waist, where the loops for the belt are, folds over every time, so if you look at me carefully while I am walking by, on the street or at the bus stop, you will see a flash of white, the cloth they use as lining, running above my belt, peeping out.

There was a time when I would have got embarrassed, tucked in my stomach, breathed deep, held that breath. Or even shouted at the tailor, refused to pay the balance, bought a firmer belt, tightened it by piercing the leather with a few extra holes. But now, why bother.

All that matters is you, my little child, and all I want at this moment is some silence so that you can sleep undisturbed and I can get over with these stories.

I will have to work fast, there isn't much time.

They are coming to take you soon, the man and the woman. They will give you everything you need; they will take you to the Alipore Zoo, to the Birla Planetarium, show you baby monkeys and mother monkeys; the tiny torchlight, shaped like an arrow, that flashes, darts across the huge black hemispherical dome. They will make faces at the monkeys, you will laugh; they will tell you where Jupiter is, why we have evening and why we have night.

And then, after several summers and several winters, when the city has fattened, its sides spilled over into the villages where the railway tracks are, where the cycle-rickshaws ply, if you grow up into the fine woman I am sure you will, one day you will stop.

Suddenly.

Something you will see or hear will remind you of something, missing in your heart, perhaps a hole, the blood rushing through it, and then like a machine which rumbles for a second just before it goes click, just before it begins to hum and move, you will stop and ask: 'Who am I?'

They will then give you these stories.

The house where we are, the room in which you sleep, is on the second floor. From the veranda, you can look down on the tram wires; the street light, the yellow sodium vapour lamp, is a couple of feet above you. If you strain your eyes, you can see dead insects trapped in the plexiglas cover. How they got in, I don't know.

Across the street, there's an oil refining mill that shut down after a workers' strike long ago. But its owner, I guess, had some of his heart still left so he continued to pay an old man to look after the dozen pigeons he kept in a cage near the entrance. Half of them are white, the rest are grey, and at least twice every day I stand in the veranda, nothing to do, watching the birds in the cage, fly around and around.

White and grey, white and grey, like tiny clouds blown across a patch of imprisoned sky.

We are on Main Circular Road, which connects the north to the south of the city, the airport to the station, and right through the day buses and trams, trucks and taxis keep passing by, making so much noise that it's only now, well past midnight, that the ringing has stopped in my ears: the horns and the brakes, the angry passengers asking the driver to please slow down or stop, bus conductors coughing and spitting, jangling the bells, shouting their destinations in between.

Now it's just the opposite, silence sits in one corner of the house, when I move my head to the right, when I move it to the left, I can hear my chin graze my collar, the sound of its stubble, I can hear my breath, even the crick in my neck, some muscle being pulled, perhaps some bone rubbing against some other bone, I am not a young man any more.

I am not going to type since the noise may wake you up, the paper being rolled in, my clumsy fingers pushing the keys, the ring at the end of each line, the paper moving up, the page ready to be rolled out.

And somewhere in the middle, if I wish to erase a word or add a letter, fix a comma, I will have to use the All-Purpose Correction Fluid. This means more noise: I will have to shake the glass bottle, open its cap, pull out the brush, let the white drop fall and then blow it dry with my lips. What if the bottle slips, falls on the floor?

At this hour, every sound gets magnified, every ear gets sharper.

I've heard that there are some babies who sleep undisturbed, even on Diwali evenings, dreaming silently to the noise of Catherine wheels and chocolate bombs. And there are some babies who wake up at the slightest of sounds, whose ears are like little funnels made of something like gossamer, ready to tremble, to catch anything in the night. A dog barking a dozen houses away, the wind blowing through the garbage dump, the ceiling fan, the tap dripping in the bathroom, the man beating his wife in the upstairs flat.

So where do I begin?

With you, the baby in my bedroom, on the blue bedspread, no taller than my arm, your tiny fingers curled up, the night resting like a soft cloud on your body. I shall begin with the phone ringing late at night, the police officer telling me that you have come into this city, unseen and unheard.

And once I have told you this story, I shall tell you more, as and when they come. I shall retell some stories, the ones your mother told me, even those which she said not in words, but in gestures and glances. Like that of the black and yellow Boroline banners catching the wind

5

on Durga Puja day; the dead pigeon, its stain carried all across the city; the albino cockroach hanging, upside down, from the bathroom drain.

Or that evening in the maternity ward, when she stood in the room, your mother, in the hospital's oversized nightdress, looking out of the window at the street lamps being switched on, one by one.

We shall visit all these places, I shall hold your hand, open all those rooms that need to be opened, word by word, sentence by sentence. I will keep some rooms closed until we are more ready, open others just a chink so that you take a peek. And at times, without opening a door at all, we shall imagine what lies inside. Like the murder, the screaming, a red handkerchief floating down, just as in the movies.

In short, I will tell you happy stories and I will tell you sad stories. And remember, my child, your truth lies somewhere in between.

POLICE STATION

'I am sorry, sir, your sister is dead.'

The telephone rings late at night, it's the Superintendent of Police, Lake Town, B Block, Calcutta 700089, Mr M. K. Chatterjee.

'I am sorry, sir,' he says, 'your sister is dead.

'We found your name written on four pages of a book she brought with her to the hospital. There was no one with her when she came in. In her admission form, she didn't write anything except her name. She was pregnant.'

I listen, I tug at the telephone cord, watch my finger push through its black spirals.

For years, I have been waiting for news of my sister. I have made up mornings and evenings, invented entire telephone calls from police stations in the night, I have looked at the crowds on TV, wondered whether it's she who walks in the top right-hand corner of the screen. Or when it rains, is she the one with the umbrella?

No, not the one with the red umbrella but the one with the black, a man's umbrella?

Sometimes, in what seems like a dream, I see a marble palace, which looks like the Victoria Memorial, where she sits on a wrought-iron bench in the garden, one leg crossed over the other, regal and lonely. Swans glide past her on the grass, white against green against the blue of the sky.

'The baby is alive,' says the police officer. 'It's a baby girl.'

What do I say?

I look around, nothing has changed. Through the window I can see two men waiting for the last tram. There's a circus in the city.

All trams have black and yellow posters plastered onto their coaches, I have been watching them all day: *Rayman Circus, Tala Park, Three shows, One, Four and Seven p.m.*

Each poster has the same woman, a small woman in a tight-fitting shining dress balancing herself on a rhino's back. And a tiger smiling, its face ringed with fire.

'Are you there, sir?' asks the police officer.

'Yes, I'm here,' I say.

'Do you know who the father is?' he asks. 'We would like to inform him. Can you tell us something about her?'

I can tell him what I am telling you: the swans, the umbrella and the TV screen, but I don't.

'I haven't seen her in a very long time,' I say.

He doesn't ask how long. 'It's very hot,' he says, 'we can't keep the body for long. If no one comes, we have to give the baby up.'

'Who will you give the baby to?' I ask.

'There's a man and a woman, a childless husband and wife, waiting for three weeks.' He pauses, I can hear him breathe, I wait.

'Police rules are police rules, sir,' he continues, 'but I can relax them a bit. It's very late in the night and I can't call them up. You can keep the baby for a day. If you decide not to keep it, I will call them.'

'Thank you,' I say.

'But you have to come down to the hospital tonight, we can't keep the body, it's very hot in here.'

It's hot, although it's December.

A full four months after the south-west monsoons have swept across the city, curved towards the Himalayas, winds laden with rain, wet and heavy, crashing against the foothills, the *Oxford University School Atlas* hung across the blackboard at school, more than twenty years ago, I can recall the oceans, the cities, a town called Genoa in Italy.

It's supposed to be cool now, that time of the year when your skin begins to dry, when you rub pomade on your elbow so that it doesn't wrinkle into a knot. One more month and on some nights in January it will get cooler, cold, so that you have to wear socks at night. But this year it's hot.

Across the road, at the bus stop, the yellow light from the street lamps falls onto the garbage dump. It's so far that I can't make out what it's falling on, I can only imagine: cracked plastic buckets, tufts of hair from the combs in the neighbourhood, women's hair, tangled and knotted, some dry, some oiled. Scraps of newspaper, fish bones, vegetable peels. Nothing new, it's been the same all these years, except that by now some of the clumps of hair have begun to grey.

'You know the way to the hospital, I hope,' he says.

'Yes,' I say.

'Please come straight to Emergency. We will be there with the baby,' says Mr Chatterjee. 'How will we recognize you?'

'I am not a young man any more, my stomach droops over the belt of my trousers.' What more can I say?

'Where?' says the taxi driver. I tell him the name of the hospital, I tell him Emergency.

'Anyone sick?' he asks. I say no, he doesn't hear, he doesn't notice, there's a black, earthen idol of a Goddess above his dashboard, two incense sticks burn, their heap of ash trembles when he changes gears.

On Grey Street, near Khanna Cinema, we take a right, past Ultadanga, the bridge, the vegetable market. The taxi's windows are rolled down, there's no one at this hour except empty wooden cots on which vendors sit every morning. I lean back and look out. High above, I can see the suburban railway station, just two platforms, the white neon sign of the Waiting Room glowing all alone. A local train sleeps, eyes wide open, stuck on the wire-mesh of the engine.

At the hospital entrance two touts run towards the taxi, they bend down, run a couple of yards, look at me. Admission? Emergency? Post-mortem? Death certificate?

I say nothing, I get out, ask the taxi driver to wait.

I walk into the Out-Patient Department, past the sick children wrapped in blankets on the floor, the saline drips propped up, along one side, the shadows of the tubes casting patterns on the wall. Two intern doctors share a cigarette, flirt with a third. A stray dog sleeps in one corner exactly like in newspaper photographs.

I see flowerpots being carried out on a stretcher, perhaps to be watered, it's very hot tonight. A nurse with two safety pins on her bangles walks past, wheeling the food tray, I see crumpled balls of aluminium foil on the hospital dinner plates, rice half-eaten. The nurse looks at me.

At the end of the hall, I see the constables, in black and white, I see you there, crying in the police officer's arms, one day old, there's a blue towel that wraps you.

Behind you, I see her lying on the trolley, covered in white.

'Can you come this side and identify her, sir?' the police officer says.

I don't need to look at her. I identify her, your mother, my sister. I sign a form, I can feel you, in my arms, cold and wet. I think I am about to cry when Mr Chatterjee, vaguely embarrassed, holds my shoulder, says I need to be brave for your sake, he helps me lift you to my face so that I can wipe my eyes in the end of the towel that wraps you. And then I walk out of the hospital. With you and the red pacifier in my pocket which the nurse gave me. 'Give this to her when she cries, when something disturbs her at night,' she says.

Nothing will disturb you at night.

My tap drips in the bathroom, I have tried many things, I have turned the steel faucet all the way to the end, turned it again, hard, harder, so hard my fingers lock on to the steel, they still hurt. But the water continues to drip on the red tiles.

We'll muffle the sound tonight, put dirty clothes below

the tap, my trousers, my shirt with the city's fingerprints on the collar and the cuff. If that doesn't work, we shall tie a handkerchief to the tap, let the water collect in the pouch, drop by drop.

The fridge also makes a noise but that's very light, as light as the old man coughing in the downstairs flat, once an hour or so. That shouldn't bother you. As for the man who beats up his wife in the upstairs flat, that must have been over by now. It's already past midnight, the husband would have gone to sleep, the wife, too, since how long will she cry?

The taxi driver pulls out of Hospital Parking, the incense sticks have burned down, some of the exhaust gets to where we sit but your eyes are closed, you are safe, in the blue towel in this city in the night.

CREMATION GROUND

*Before we make our first trip to the past, let us go to the
future, to a day, many years from now, when you are in
a room with several people. As soon as you turn, maybe
to get a glass of water or to look out of the window, they
point you out with their eyes which say:*

*Don't you know she is the one who came out of her
mother's womb, leaving her mother dead?*

*Do you know who brought her from the hospital? Her
mother's brother who didn't even cry that night. Not one
tear drop? No.*

Unknown to them, you see what they say.

*Will you keep your back turned, angry and hurt? Or
will you put on a smile, walk straight into their waiting
arms, into their trap of pity? I don't know.*

*All I know is that in this city of twelve million, if six
or seven, even ten people, say words that hurt, they are a
speck in the ocean. Wait for a while, the moon will slide
into the right place, the clouds will gather, there will*

*come a tide and with it a wave which will wash this
speck away.*

The exhaust gets into our eyes, the driver rolls up the
windows, the black sunfilm on the glass is chipped in
several places but that's not enough for the city's light to
enter the taxi. So we are moving in the dark, the inside
lit only by the light from the dashboard, trapped behind
the half-broken dials. It's a weak light, it dies before it
can cross the front seat.

Let the city pass us tonight because it has nothing to
show, no longer does it have your mother, my sister. We
shall not roll the windows down, the hospital building
gets smaller and smaller behind us, there's no need to
turn and look back.

To our right is the market, closed at this time but even
if it were open, even if there were women, trying out earrings, looking into mirrors held in their hands, choosing
blouses that match with their saris, buying handkerchiefs
for their husbands, three coloured, three in checks, I
wouldn't have looked.

For now we are sure, none of those women will be
your mother.

To our left is the new flyover that leads to the airport,
two lanes on either side, separated by a concrete divider

along which they have put little plants in wire cages, all waiting to be trees. So far, I have only seen the flyover in the newspaper, these plants, the giant halogen lamps that change night into day, the reflectors, bought from Japan, dividing the lanes, but tonight we won't look at all this.

Because even if there's a beautiful woman, all alone, walking down the flyover's ramp that merges with the main road, it doesn't matter. We know she cannot be your mother.

Your mother is dead, she was cremated an hour ago.

If this city were flat, if all buildings were only as high as the people inside, if all the lights were switched off, the sky washed clean, the factories gone to sleep, we could have seen the smoke from her pyre. I would then have made an exception, rolled the taxi's windows down, let some of the smoke glide past you, your mother's last touch.

They lift her off the trolley, slide her into a stretcher, the white sheet still covers all of her, and they walk past the Out-Patient Department into the lobby where the neon lights spell out the hospital's name.

They put her down, four people, one in each corner of the stretcher, three strangers and I.

'We'll arrange the van, sir,' says one. 'Let's get it over with tonight itself, why wait?'

'Do you have some money with you?' asks another. 'We may have to pay extra for the wood.'

'Yes,' I say. 'How long will it take?'

'Not long,' he says. 'At this time, there aren't many people. Most wait for the morning.'

The van is white, its rear doors open, the hospital's huge red cross split into two halves, like pieces in some sad jigsaw puzzle. They slide the stretcher into the back, on the floor, between the two seats.

Her sheet has slid off half of her left foot, her toe is exposed, I can see the nail, still clear and neatly cut, reflect some light coming from the outside, maybe a street lamp. A passing vehicle's headlights.

I want to look at her face, I don't want to look at her face.

We must have passed the flyover now, without looking out I know. Since its halogen lights are far behind us, the inside of the taxi is darker, much darker.

I'll see the flyover some day, especially the little plants in their cages, waiting to be trees. If the rains come to the city on time, if the sun shines as long as it should, these plants will not have to wait for long.

What kind of trees will these be? Not the eucalyptus, like in the hospital compound, not the one with flowers, like in the park, nor the banyan across our house. These will be nameless trees in a concrete garden. And below these trees will live nameless people who will gather in a flock, head for the landfill at Tangra, and like birds who pick up things for their nests, one twig at a time, they will gather, for their houses, tarpaulin, bricks, strong nylon rope, sometimes even something to adorn, like a broken doll or a calendar, its pictures not yet torn.

'Ten more minutes, sir,' says the taxi driver.

This should be Main Circular Road, we are about to reach, the taxi shudders, we are now on the tramlines, the taxi slows down, below us are the cobbled tracks, the potholes caused by the rains that wash away the concrete and it's only many months later that the Calcutta Corporation people come, with rollers and huge drums, they switch it on and work the entire night, lighting fires, mixing stone chips to make the tar which will then be carried in black buckets and poured into the holes.

Two boys jump out of the shadows, run to the van as soon as we enter, the hospital men tell them to clear off, we walk down the steps to the yard where they have marked out the rectangles for the pyres.

'Wait there, we will get the wood,' says one.

I wait, the river is one big black table top glistening in the dark. Far away I can see the steamers, their lanterns flickering, the dark shapes of the Howrah Bridge, there is one pyre to my left that has burnt down, must be at least two hours ago, because there are no embers left, no smoke, just ash, its heat coming to me in waves.

She is ready now, the sheet still on her, the toe now covered, a priest comes from nowhere. 'One hundred rupees,' he says, and then stands beside me.

I put you down on the bed, place two pillows on either side, to rest against your tiny hands, each smaller than my finger. The time has come, I go to my room, take out the paper, they placed the wood on her body, one log at a time, the thick ones at the bottom, the thin ones at the top, I have had these sheets of paper for quite some time, the ones at the top are yellow at the edges, the ones below are still white and crisp, the priest asked me to hold the splinter and walk around the pyre, I could begin with my name but why waste time, she begins to burn, they poured oil, the wood made noises, the van was lit by her flames, I write about my trousers, their white lining, the smoke gets into my eyes. There isn't much time, the man and the woman are coming to take you tomorrow, the fire was still burning when we left, let me tell you about the doctor with arms as white as milk, I am seven years old, she was gone, you were waiting at the hospital, why should I cry.

THE BOY AND THE DOG

Sitting, the shade partial woman, any size. There isn't much time, the fire is pushing, coming to take you... you will not this moment by him... in seven years out, the boy goes you... I hoped someone could...

Still Life

✦⊶⊷✦

Three stories and you haven't cried, I have to get up to check.

I walk on my toes, I hold my breath. My slippers go slap-slap on the cement floor; when I inhale, the air and my body make a noise, when I walk at this time of the night, you can hear my arms rub against my white nightshirt. I have to be careful.

The door to your bedroom creaks. Its hinges have moved, opening and closing, about four or five times a day, three hundred and sixty-five days a year, thirty years. At the bottom of the door, the edge is chipped, a sharp sliver of wood has given way, it scrapes the floor every time the door moves.

That's the sound which puts me on the edge, I don't want you to hear it. So I spend one full minute pushing the door, millimetre by millimetre, until it opens. Just enough, about a foot, for me to pass. And I see you haven't moved in your sleep.

The two pillows I propped up on either side of you are exactly as they were. I used my hands to fluff one pillow, the hollows my fingers left are still there. I stand by your bed and watch you, your tiny hands, each smaller than my little finger, the night draped over your head.

I bend down to look at you closely, the fragrance of your new life comes rushing to me, I blow gently in your two-day-old hair, you still don't move.

You are like your mother.

When she slept, it was as if she had walked into a photograph and then never came out of the glass frame the entire night. Even if her arm was caught in an awkward angle, even if her head was half on the pillow, half outside, and her neck hurt, it didn't matter.

Her hair across the pillow stayed exactly the way it fell when she first closed her eyes. It was only on some summer nights, when I got up, covered with sweat, to turn the fan's regulator from two to three to four, sometimes even five, that her hair moved. Caught in the sudden rush of air, it rustled over the pillow, brushed my face like thin feathers in the dark.

But she didn't move.

*

Once, I asked her why. She laughed, she said there was no reason, some people move in their sleep, some don't.

I asked her again, she laughed again. Until one night, just before going to sleep, she told me to close the door, switch the lights off and then she whispered why.

There is this dream I have every night, she said. Sometimes, it's the first dream of the night, sometimes it comes in between two dreams, and sometimes it's played out in slow motion, lasting the entire night.

It's early winter in the city, the air is cool, I am in a park, which park I don't know. It's very quiet, I can't hear any buses or trams, even people. There's fine green grass on the ground, like in front of the Victoria Memorial, the wind is light, I can feel it in my hair, on the grass.

I sit on a wrought-iron bench, in front of a marble palace. Swans glide past me on the grass, white against green against the blue of the sky. And about ten feet away from me, sits a man, his face covered by a large rectangular canvas propped up on a dark brown wooden stand.

It's like in the pictures of artists in story books. I can't see him in full, I see only a flash of his elbow when he moves his hands, I can see his knee, he's wearing dark trousers. His face I can't see.

Once or twice, he bends to his left to look at me, to check if he's getting the lines right, but I cannot remember his face. All I remember is what he tells me from behind the canvas. One sentence, at least three or four times: 'Don't move,' he says, 'I am painting you, please don't move.'

Maybe that's why I don't move in my sleep, she said.

FATHER

STAMMERING CLINIC

'What do you see?' the doctor asks.

'There's a street lamp,' I say. 'And there's an empty road. There are small houses on either side. They are coloured red, green, blue, silver and yellow. Each house has two windows and a door.'

'Who do you think lives there?'

'People,' I say.

'What kind of people?'

'Rabbits and bears, pixies and gnomes like in the story book where the faraway trees whisper wisha wisha wisha at night.'

'Good boy,' she says.

It takes me half an hour to say all this and by the time I'm done, I have fallen off the chair, I lie on the carpet, my chest hurts, my ears are burning, my eyes are wet with tears.

She gives me a glass of water, offers her hand, helps me get up. She's a beautiful woman, the doctor, much more beautiful than my class teacher Miss Constance Lopez. She wears a sleeveless blue blouse, her bare arms are as white as the milk I have for breakfast. Her sari is red with black flowers all over.

It's a July afternoon, three days before my seventh birthday, the rain's coming down in sheets so thick that the black umbrella buckles under its weight. We are travelling in a taxi, my father and I, to the doctor, who has her chambers in a white building on Russell Street near Jamuna Cinema.

The driver has rolled up the windows but they don't go the entire way, they don't close tight and through the four horizontal cracks at the top, between the glass and the window frame, the rain keeps squeezing in with the wind.

So we keep moving away from the windows until we sit real close, Father and I, like two friends huddled in the rain.

It's the day after the Parent–Teacher meeting in which Miss Lopez suggested that Father take me to the white building on Russell Street near Jamuna Cinema so that I got cured.

'He's a nice boy,' she said. 'He needs to get over this thing,' and she ran her hand through my hair as if she were looking for a place, a soft place in my head. 'Usually, parents can be of great help in all this, they can make a great difference,' she says.

And Father looks at her, then looks sideways at the blackboard where there's nothing, no teaching today, except for a world map rolled up. I keep looking at the stapler and the Scotch tape on Miss Lopez's desk, feeling Father's guilt pushing at me.

'I'll certainly take him there, Miss Lopez,' says Father. 'You are right.'

It's an apartment building, as in American films, Venetian blinds on windows, complete with a lobby and an elevator, plants lined up along the wall. There is a brass plate with names written, who is on which floor. There is a guard, in a blue suit, his buckles shine, he is also wearing a cap and he's watching the rain drum on the steps that lead to his chair. He asks Father where we are going and Father shows him something written on a piece of paper and he points to the stairs. Third floor, he says.

We climb the stairs up to the third floor where it's

quiet and dry. Father looks funny in his raincoat, my hair is wet, I can feel the rain squeak between my toes in my shoes.

We wait in the lobby, dripping onto the green carpet. Once again, like in the taxi, we keep moving from one place on the sofa to another so that the carpet doesn't get all wet in one place. We are embarrassed but it doesn't matter since there's no one present, just two red sofas that stretch from one end of the wall to the other. And a money plant in the middle of the room.

I cannot recall how long we waited but it must have been quite a while since we were dry when she walked in and I had begun to shiver a bit. We were the only two people in the lobby.

She brings out a book, a brightly coloured book. It must have been printed in a foreign country since the colours are bright and sharp, the pages so smooth they reflect the light from her table lamp.

'What do you see?' she says.

There's a street lamp, I say, and there's an empty road. There are small houses on either side. I stop, my chest heaves, I can feel the breath driving through me like an express train. They are coloured red, green, blue, silver and yellow. I am trembling now, Father is looking at me one moment, at the table lamp the next. Each house has two windows and a door, I say.

I am lying on the carpet, the words grow and grow until they fill up my lungs and refuse to come out, they gulp down my breath making my lips quiver like in winter.

Father offers me his hand, I hold it and get up. She gives me another glass of water, this time it's chilled, she turns the page of the book.

Now I can see two pigeons flying, their wings half-covering the setting sun between brown hills. There's a lake with a girl rowing in a boat, her pigtails so long they almost touch their reflections in the water. There's a little red fish staring at the girl, its body speckled with tiny black stars.

'You don't have to say it this time,' she says, tearing a page from her exercise book.

It's like the sketchbook in school, with neither squares nor lines. Blank and white, nothing to guide you as you write or draw. The paper isn't exactly white, it's rough, some expensive kind of parchment I have never seen before.

'Write it down,' she says and puts her arm around me,

I can smell her perfume, like milk chocolate mixed with roses, the red of her sari against my eyes through which I can see Father restless on the sofa looking the other way.

I write down what I see and she reads it, she tells me to fold the piece of paper and put it in my pocket and take it home.

When we step out, the rain has stopped, the streets are flooded. Father rolls up his trousers, I remove my shoes and we walk, the city's grime lapping against us, my wet shoes like two little black kittens I am holding by their necks.

'Careful,' says Father. 'Give me the paper on which you wrote. I don't want it to get wet.'

I give it to him and he puts it in his shirt pocket, high up, more than five feet above the street. 'Water can't reach here,' he says and he smiles. 'Let's go, we don't have to come here again.'

'Why?' I ask.

He doesn't answer, just walks ahead, and I follow him, looking down, looking at the deep brown water mixed with gasoline cut itself in V-shaped wakes whenever a vehicle passes us by, Father's calves are wet, the hair all neatly lined up.

And perhaps it was on that rain-flooded afternoon,

when I turned back to look at the white building on Russell Street for the last time that I understood what seems to be the most important lesson my Father taught me: when you find it difficult to say something, when the words get trapped in your chest, your lips quiver, as in winter, you can always write it down. That's why, my child, I have nothing to worry about tonight, I am prepared.

ONE RUPEE

Bhabani, the maid, and I are standing outside the door which Father has locked from the inside and we can hear him beating my sister. Someone is on the bed, someone is on the floor. The person on the bed is running, I think it's Sister because the creaks are gentle. The bed is very old, my sister says Mother got it from her father when she got married.

My sister is four years elder to me, we go to the same school, she is in Class VIII A, I am in Class V B. Her teacher is Mr Peter D'Souza, mine is Miss Constance Lopez. Mr D'Souza wears a very nice cologne, Miss Lopez's son died in a shipwreck near Australia. He had gone there on a vacation with his friends and the ship sank. I have read about Australia, the Great Barrier Reef, the Flying Doctor, I like Miss Lopez a lot.

Why is Father beating my sister? To tell you the

answer, I have to tell you about what happened in school today.

I am a very good student, I come first in my class, the boy who comes second is very good in Mathematics and Science but I always beat him in Second Language. I do very well in Hindi and get at least eighty-five. He is not so good in Bengali, which is his Second Language, and gets at the most seventy. So that means I get fifteen marks extra there, he beats me in Mathematics by seven to eight marks and Science by two to three which doesn't add up and this is how I come first.

Once, he beat me in Science by twenty marks and he came first. Father got very angry. My sister is a good student too, she comes sixth or seventh in her class, she doesn't like to study. She doesn't need to study, she's very intelligent, she remembers everything by heart.

Every day, Father gives my sister two rupees. I am very young and that is why I am not allowed to keep any money with me. The bus ticket is forty paise. So every day, we spend forty into four, one rupee sixty paise. We save forty paise. Father doesn't ask for this. After five days, we save two rupees and then my sister and I have a vanilla ice cream each.

There are students in my class who don't have to wait for five days, who eat ice cream every day, expensive ice creams, the kind which comes in biscuit cones or plastic cups. They are rich students but because I come first in my class and because my sister is very beautiful they all come to me for help before the exams. Maybe that's why I don't feel so bad.

Today, while going to school, Father didn't have change so he gave my sister a five-rupee note. It was already ten minutes to eight and it takes about twenty minutes to reach school. We have to be there by quarter past eight, in time for the Assembly when Sister Lucy, who is from Ireland and who is our principal, starts the prayers. *God make me a channel of your peace, an instrument of your love.*

If we are late, we have to wait outside her office with our green diaries and at eight forty she comes back and is very angry. Her assistant, Miss Elisa Gomes, first stamps our diaries: Permission to attend classes LATE granted. And then with our diaries opened to that page we wait outside her office, all of us who have come late. Sister Lucy calls us in, without looking at us, one by one, and while she's signing our diaries, she asks us why we are late. We always tell her that the bus was late. Or that there was a big jam on Amherst Street. She doesn't know much about buses.

I like to stand near the Ladies' Seat because there are two girls who go to school, not my school, who are usually on the same bus. They have smart uniform: chocolate-coloured skirts and white shirts.

One girl is very studious, she's always reading a book which she keeps covered with brown paper. It's not a textbook, it's small, the size of a story book, and I don't know what she reads. It must be a mystery book since she never once looks up, even if the bus brakes suddenly. I like her reading the book because she has short hair which falls across her face when she reads and it looks very nice.

The other girl is not the studious type. She's fashionable, she wears a shorter skirt and, at times, I have also seen her in a sleeveless shirt. She is not as beautiful as my sister but I like to watch her and I think I am in love with her. When I get married, I want my wife to be like her.

One day, she was carrying a Laboratory notebook and I saw her name on the cover: Geeti.

Maybe it was her friend's notebook but I now always

think of her as Geeti. Her arms have two tiny vaccination marks which we all have but which look extra good on her, her knees are also very smooth and they shine when light falls through the window. At times, when she turns to look out of the window, her legs turn and because her skirt is short, I can also see her thigh. Then I look the other way. I don't want to make her self-conscious.

When we boarded the bus today, Geeti was not there. The studious girl was standing, the bus was really crowded since these two girls always get seats.

My sister gave the five-rupee note to the conductor who gave her two tickets and said he would give the change later. My sister then walked through the crowd in the bus to the centre.

I don't know why she does this but she always does this. She's very bold, like a grown-up boy. I stand near the exit door so that when the school stop comes I can get down fast. On days if I get a seat which is far away from the door and the bus is crowded, I get up two stops in advance and start walking towards the door. But my sister is the exact opposite.

Even when the bus is packed, she pushes her way through the people until she reaches the centre of the bus. And if she gets a seat, she will get up only at the last moment, just when the bus is about to stop near the school. One of these days, I think, she won't be able to get down and the bus will take her all the way to Chowringhee.

Today, she did the same thing. She walked to the centre and the bus was so crowded that after five minutes I couldn't even see her. So I stood there, packed between several people, I could smell their sweat, they were so close, but I just stood there, fixed, always looking through the window because I didn't want to miss the school stop.

The conductor calls the stops aloud but I want to be sure. Bank of India, Bowbazar. Bowbazar is our stop from where the bus turns. Just before reaching Bank of India, there's a very big hospital, the Lady Dufferin College and Hospital, with a very, very long boundary wall, red in colour. If I am standing in the bus, I keep looking through the window and when that red wall comes into my view, I know it's time to start walking towards the door.

When I got down, the conductor gave me the change since my sister had gotten down from the door in front. The conductor gave me four one-rupee coins and twenty paise. We started running because the clock on top of the

Bowbazar market showed eight fifteen already. Only five minutes to reach the classroom, dump the bag and run downstairs for the Assembly.

Just as we entered the school, the first bell rang. We were both running, my sister and I, when I remembered that I had the change from the bus and I stopped, I wasn't supposed to carry any money and so I gave her all the coins I had.

During the lunch recess, I stood in the veranda, in front of my classroom, talking to my friend Chetan Shah, who has broken his arm and it has been two weeks but he still has a cast.

He is a very rich boy because he comes in a car and always gets cheese for lunch, triangular cheese wrapped in shiny paper. His father has a toy shop on Park Street and he tells me all about the latest toys that have come. On my birthday this year, he gave me a Rubik's cube. I am not very good with it.

I was talking to Chetan and I don't exactly know what happened but I had my hand in my pocket and I was about to take out my handkerchief when I felt it. It was a one-rupee coin. By God, I got frightened.

*

Whose money was this? Where had the one-rupee coin come from? I didn't know, I was scared. Father would be very angry if he saw me with money. I am not supposed to keep any money with me, money is bad. What do I do? All sorts of questions went round and round in my head. Chetan had gone downstairs to drink water and I was very frightened. So I took the coin, looked all around but no one was watching, and threw it as far as I could. Into the playground, I saw the coin land, fall in the grass, I saw a bit of it shining in the sun but only for a moment because when I looked away and turned to look at it for a second time, I couldn't see it any more. It had vanished into the grass.

Classes began, we had Geography, Art and English, the story about Uncle Podger hanging a picture, I forgot all about the coin until I reached home and in the evening when Father came back from work and checked our school diaries, he asked my sister for the change. She went to her bag and gave Father all the change she had. One rupee was missing.

I promise, it didn't strike me, that feeling in my pocket, Chetan going down to drink water, me throwing the coin into the playground, watching it land. I know it sounds as if I'm lying but at that time I forgot that the missing coin had been in my pocket and that I had thrown it away because I was afraid.

'Where is the one rupee?' Father said and my sister said she didn't know. Father got angry, angrier.

First, he slapped my sister, like he often does. A slap on her cheek, my sister is a very, very brave girl and she never cries when Father beats her. This makes Father more angry and he beats her harder but she just stands there, like a statue, until he gives up and says that his hands hurt.

But this time Father got very angry, he kept on shouting and sister went to the next room. He followed her and locked the door from the inside, Bhabani heard and came running from the kitchen. A few minutes later, we heard the noises coming from that room, Father's angry shouts and my sister running, dodging him as the slaps fell on her.

She runs, she crashes against the dressing table and the powder box, the combs fall, we can hear the sound. Bhabani shouts that one rupee is not such a big thing and she tells Father to stop because everybody in the building can hear him. She says that if he doesn't have any love, he should at least have some shame.

*

It's then that it all comes back, the crowd in the bus, I'm getting down, the conductor gives me the change, the time on the clock, I give the coins back to my sister, one coin remains in my pocket, the lunch, Chetan, I find the coin and throw it away. It is my fault and Sister doesn't know.

But Father is so angry and I am so scared that I can't tell him all this now. Not once does Sister tell him that it was I who got the change from the conductor today. She remembers everything by heart, she doesn't remember I could have made a mistake.

My sister goes to sleep without eating dinner, she always does that when she's angry and hurt. There are marks on her face where Father hit her. She will now have to stay home for a few days until the marks disappear. I also don't eat dinner, I say my stomach hurts, that's the least I can do.

We are lying in bed, Bhabani has switched off the lights, from the drawing room, we can hear the clock ticking. And when she is alone with me, Sister begins to cry, her face turned towards the wall. Through her tears, she asks me, 'What happened to the one-rupee coin?'

I don't know what to do, I don't say anything.

'Do you remember how much you gave me?' she asks.

I don't say anything.

The night closes in on me, I close my eyes tight, I lie awake as she cries to sleep, hurt and hungry. I keep looking at the wall on which I can see big, scary patterns from the headlights of the trucks outside.

The next morning came and the next and the next, winter came, my sister never once talked about that evening, that one-rupee coin, the English team arrived, led by Tony Greig, who was so tall his bat didn't touch the ground, our bowlers dropped several catches, it was the year they had begun showing the matches on TV.

Geeti began wearing a bra, letting one strap peek from under her top across her shoulder.

Milestones, landmarks, passed us by.

Today, almost everything inside me has stopped growing except the guilt of that afternoon. Like a monster which gets its endless supply of food and water from some place we shall never know, it keeps growing and growing inside me every day and all I can do is to wait for it to swallow me whole.

GARDEN CHILD

At a different time, maybe at a different place, I would have told you other stories. Of the two Alsatian dogs in the neighbourhood who bit into our cricket balls until we poisoned them one night. Of the different ways in which our neighbourhood has changed, so many you can't count them on your fingers: how the road, on either side of the tram tracks, has widened, a twenty-four-hour telephone booth, with glass cubicles, has sprouted at the street corner. How Bhar And Sons, the shop which once sold iron rods, is now the local cable centre, satellite dishes sit atop its asbestos roof, cable wires sag across its sky.

Plus a lot more, I would have twisted fact, fleshed out fiction, but tonight, looking at the darkness looking at me through the window, there's only one image that emerges, like a photograph half-processed, in the yellow light of the table lamp in my room.

It's the image of a child lying, on his stomach, in a tiny

garden, his elbows making two hollows in the damp earth, his fingers pressed like sepals against his face. There's no one beside him, just a parallelogram of light that falls on the grass from a large window.

Who is this child, it's not clear, all I know is that this story will have a happy ending.

I close my eyes and concentrate; so hard they prise free from the sockets and I let them fly across the room. Dodging below the fan, in between the bookshelves, through the green window, past the red curtains, down into the street. In and out of the traffic, inside a tram, around the passengers, some sitting some standing.

Across Esplanade, past the beauty salon on Park Street where two Chinese women in black jeans wait for customers; across the Maidan, carried on by the breeze, through the trees cold and quivering.

I concentrate harder; let the eyes glide over the Hooghly, briskly skim its black surface, barely touching the buffaloes that wallow, their snouts above the water. Below the bridge, into the railway station, over the crowd, the vendors running with their trolleys, into the train that's pulling out of the platform. They flit from one coach to the next, up and down the berths, left and right of the aisle, watching and looking until the eyes see the child, one hand across his face, trying to sleep.

His mother sleeps on the berth below, his father sits at her feet reading a newspaper. Maybe it's the light in the coach, the two green lamps directly overhead that stare at him through their wire cages and keep him from falling asleep. The child turns over so that his back faces the lamps, his legs are curled up, his bare feet pressed against each other. The train gathers speed, rattles and whines, crosses the suburbs, the railway quarters rush by in streaks of red, yellow and blue light.

A lone vendor totters down the aisle, hawking ball-point pens, red, black and blue.

My eyes cross over the child to that two-inch gap between him and the wall and there I can see a large window with the wind billowing the curtains.

It's late at night and the child is lying, on his stomach, in the tiny garden, his elbows making two hollows in the damp earth, his fingers pressed like sepals against his face. He is looking at the window and when the curtain rises, in that fleeting moment before it falls with the wind, he sees his mother standing in the centre of the room, father sitting in a black chair, his legs raised on the black table, reading a book.

He cannot make out what his parents are saying, Father's head is lowered, perhaps he is reading aloud. Mother interjects with a laugh but Father goes on. Words, weighed down by his heavy voice, float down, disjointed, from the window.

Mother laughs again; the darkness around the child seems to melt and from far away he can faintly hear the No. 12 tram trundling towards the Galiff Street terminus. It must be around midnight. Two hours past his bedtime but there's no sleep tonight as he keeps looking at the window, watching Father read to Mother, listening to the hiss of crickets, a distant car horn.

Behind him roll the plots of empty West Bengal Housing Board land, several dug up, some covered with barbed wire wrapped around sheets of corrugated tin, others with tiny hills of black stone chips, iron rods and bags of cement.

Something brushes the nape of his neck, he brushes it off. It is a black ant, now wriggling in his palm trying to flip over and crawl through the gap between his fingers. He raises his palm to his face, blows the ant away, watches it sail across the night to land on a leaf, un-harmed. And it's during this moment of distraction, lasting barely fifteen seconds, when his eyes are off the window, when the ant is in flight, that the scene shifts as if in a movie.

Father beats Mother.

The curtains continue to rise and fall, the wind still blows in a steady breath but now Father is standing close to Mother, the book still in his hand. The child watches the hand rise, Mother not move, the book come crashing against her head. She lurches back, half stumbles, bal-ances herself. Father steps back, doesn't throw the book at the wall, just lets it fall. His hand now free, he moves closer, pulls Mother up by her hair.

In the garden now there are several sounds: the chair being pushed and then toppling over, the screech of the table's legs against the floor, Mother's bangles cracking and both Father and Mother crashing against the table lamp, their shadows flitting across the wall and then flowing into the ceiling.

And then, as suddenly as it began, it's all over. Silence rushes in to fill the cracks in the night.

Father is gone and Mother, perhaps, is still there lying on the floor. The curtains, as always, rise and fall and the child continues to look at the window, this time bent and curved, through the water in his eyes.

I could tell you more about the child, more about that night, what happened when the child returned to his room. How long it took for him to fall asleep and when he did, what dreams did he dream. But those are frills, details needed merely to fill the blanks of my memory.

As of now, however, let's not waste time, let us look forward, perhaps a few months later, at the child as he lies on the upper berth of an express train speeding through the night, knowing full well that this is one night his mother is safe.

For, although Father still looks menacing, the newspaper in his hand, his elbows inches away from Mother's feet, he cannot touch her. There are other passengers in the coach, many still awake; there's the vendor with his ballpoint pens walking up and down the aisle and it's this heavenly comfort of strangers which the child covers himself with. Like a soft, warm quilt in January.

Someone switches off the overhead lights but that doesn't seem to matter. He can hear the shuffle of feet as someone walks to the lavatory. He turns over to look at the hollow of darkness below, between the two rows of berths.

When his eyes adjust, he can see, in the pale shadows cast by the suitcases and the trunks stacked below, shreds of newsprint, soft-drink straws, groundnut shells and smudges of water on the floor. Across the aisle, a middle-aged man is looking through the window, eating something out of a paper plate, his white plastic water-bottle with the blue cap swaying in gentle arcs from the hook above.

Outside, night rushes by broken only by the silhouettes of trees, near and far, fast and slow.

I could end the story here but that would leave it for ever trapped in the past, incomplete and purposeless.

So let's imagine that the child grows up, leaves this city, travels to faraway places, meets people, falls in love, gets married and returns to live perhaps in that same house with the tiny garden in front.

Let's make the house older, but not sadder, although large chunks of it have cracked, marked by long jagged lines, green and brown, caused by the rains in July and August. Across the street, the plots of land are in full bloom, rows and rows of apartment buildings, each with its little window, little balcony and a fat black water tank.

And in the evenings when they switch the lights on in these apartments, when these countless rectangles of light overpower the gathering darkness of twilight, let him sit in the same black chair, his legs raised on the same black table.

He reads aloud to his wife; outside, their child lies on his stomach, in the garden, staring at the window, his elbows making two hollows in the damp earth, his fingers pressed like sepals against his face. The curtains billow in the wind, Mother laughs and interjects, while in the other room, the television keeps talking to no one in particular.

They have an argument, their voices rise. And this time, Father gets up, puts the book on the table, his shadow on the wall, walks first to his wife, kisses her on the nose, she makes a face, smiles, and then he walks to the window, calls out to the child, pulling his little family into a world he has only now begun to explore.

BLUE BEDSPREAD

The bedspread was ten feet by nine feet, dark blue,
almost purple, but over the years it had faded until it was
bluish-white, like our breakfast of milk and cornflakes.
When we returned from school in the afternoon, we
would lie on the bed, Sister and I, our cheeks pressed
against the thick fabric, our eyes fixed along the surface,
imagining we were looking at the sky. And that the
discoloured patches were clouds.

At night we turned off the lights and before our eyes
could adjust to the darkness all around my sister would
switch on the bedside lamp. Its shade was made of cane
and through its slats the light fell in a hundred specks
on the bedspread making our black sky shimmer with
stars. Sister would then lean over and spin the shade,
making it revolve slowly around the light bulb so that
the stars would begin to move in huge orbits across the
bed.

We did this every night except when the bedspread

was due for washing, once every ten days. Then it would lie in the red plastic bucket in the bathroom, drowned in mugs and mugs of water and soap. My sister and I took turns visiting the bathroom to look at our sky, crumpled and wet, jammed into the bucket so hard we were afraid the clouds would crack.

In the morning the soap suds would have disappeared leaving the water a dirty brown and Bhabani, the maid, would hitch her sari above her knees and begin pounding the bedspread with the wooden mallet I often used as a cricket bat. That booming sound, reflected off the walls of the bathroom, was our morning music to which we waltzed through the arduous rituals of preparing for school. When she was done, we would help her carry it up to the terrace, the bedspread all wet and gleaming like the velvet curtain of a cinema hall, and we left for school safe in the realization that when we would return, our sky would be back, fresh and clean.

I don't remember how long my sister and I went on with this little secret game. She was fourteen, I was ten, and it was on our ninety square feet of fabric sky that we first kissed and, later, touched each other in what then we thought were the wrong places. And it was this daily theatre of pleasure and fear, played out on our blue bedspread, that carried us as if on a wave from one night to the next.

For a moment, after we had bolted the door, nothing seemed to matter. Neither Father sleeping in the adjacent room nor Mother staring at us from a giant photograph behind the lamp, two dead cockroaches trapped in its glass frame. Just the stars caressing our bodies, lying still in the darkness, the only sound our two hearts, and sometimes a Bengal–Bihar cargo truck rumbling by.

And then one July evening, when it had rained right through the day, our secret was laid bare.

I returned from school drenched, my exercise books wet at the corners; my shoes cold and heavy, like the tiny black boats fished out of the river. Sister spread the books out on the bedspread, turned the fan to maximum, dried my hair with a towel and propped my shoes on either side of the gas stove. By evening, the books had dried, their pages flapped in the fan's draft. The shoes had begun to steam, making the house smell of leather and rain when Father came home drunk and laughing.

Whenever Father was drunk and laughing, he would do stupid things: once, he took a kitchen knife and flushed it down the toilet. The knife got stuck, the water stopped flowing and for two mornings before the plumber arrived Sister and I kept our legs crossed as we prayed hard hoping that we didn't spoil our pants. Later, that was to become one of our few family jokes: if we could hold our shit for two days, we could hold down anything in the world.

At other times Father would hide Sister's sanitary napkins so that she was forced to borrow my handkerchief. Sometimes he would become violent and shave himself with neither soap nor water until he bled. It was at those times that we got frightened. My sister was a strong woman; she would grasp his shoulders and shake him, sometimes even slap him hard. He would then start crying and slowly slide down the sofa; his eyes would remain half-open and he would fall asleep.

That evening when Father came home Sister was away. She had gone to the British Council to return some books which were long overdue. Father smiled and said he wanted to see me naked. 'Let's see how grown up you are now,' he said. At first, I thought it was yet another of his drunken jokes, but then he stood there in the middle of the bedroom, the smile melting away, and told me that he knew what Sister and I were up to at night. If I didn't undress, he said, he would tell Sister all about it. Or better still, make us sleep in different rooms.

I kept listening, the battle had been lost, I kept staring at the patches of rain on the wall: a rabbit with an ear missing, a dog its tail.

Maybe I should have protested but that afternoon, with Father drunk and laughing, with Sister gone and my only secret lying suddenly exposed, I closed my eyes, undressed and on Father's orders lay on the blue bedspread.

It was cold, the rain from the exercise books had seeped into the fabric. I could hear the sound of cars splashing the water in the potholes outside, I could hear the minibus conductors shout their destinations: Dum Dum, Howrah, Entally, Roxy Cinema.

Someone laughed from the street outside; I think I shouted, I'm not sure. Even if I had, my scream wouldn't have gone beyond the places where buses go.

What happened later is split, torn, and then welded together, as if in a dream. I fell asleep; I remember that when I woke up, the buses had long gone, the rain had stopped leaving the street gleaming like Sister's hair. I stood in the tiny balcony overlooking the street, I can recall crying.

However, what I remember more than the tears is the view of the street lamps through water-filled eyes: the white neon light bent and curved, split into its component colours. Through the blur of that spectrum, I could see the oil mill across the street, soft and diffuse as if in a magazine photograph. The red flags strung across its entrance drooped limp and wet in the rain. I must have stood there for quite some time since my legs had begun to hurt. I was also beginning to panic: I hadn't done my geography homework.

By the time Sister announced that dinner was ready, the tears had dried. At the dining table, I tried to hide behind the glass of milk watching Father and Sister eat silently. I wanted to shrink, climb up the glass and dive down to its bottom, swim in circles, let the milk's whiteness fill my body, wash the stickiness and some blood away.

'You don't have to go to school tomorrow,' Father said, standing at the sink washing his hands.

'You look unwell,' he said, lighting a cigarette, walking up to the table and holding me close. I could hear the dinner in his stomach, my heart pressed against his groin.

*

That night, my sister didn't switch on the bedside lamp. And with all the stars locked in the blackness of the bedroom, we held each other tight. The bedspread was dank from the rain, stained and crusted where the come had slipped off my legs. But my sister didn't seem to notice as she lay, not speaking a word, her red shirt rolled up to allow my lips to shelter her nipple, my chin to rest on the small pillow of her breast and my hands pressed, warm and soft, between her legs.

We could hear Father snore in the next room, the rattle of the windows whenever a huge Bengal–Bihar cargo truck rumbled by. Light from the street filtered through the frosted glass panes making Sister's hair shine. I could feel the rise and fall of her breasts, hear the gentle rush of her breathing.

She had fallen asleep, so I withdrew my hands, rolled her shirt back to her waist, pulled the covers over her and snuggled close. She turned in her sleep but she didn't let me go and my head came to fit exactly in the curve of her neck, her arms came to rest across my back.

I lay there awake, staring at the darkness so comfortably nestled between our bodies, allowing it to wash my eyes, lull me to sleep. And although my body still hurt, where Father had put his entire weight on that evening, I kept drowning in a stream, a river and then an ocean of happiness.

That night happened more than twenty-five years ago. I have embellished Father's heavy breathing, my muffled screams, with adjectives in my mind. I have made Father's trousers black at one time, blue at another; changed that rainy evening to a hot summer morning. Or when I have felt like it, I have made it pour that night so that Sister and I, locked in embrace, can hear the drops drum against the window.

As for my sister, she walked out of home when she was nineteen with someone I hope she loved.

For quite some time, several years, I missed her as if I had walked out of an operating theatre, cured but with something missing, something that had been an integral part of me, the absence of which I would feel every waking moment.

And then, slowly, like sunrise on a winter's day, it dawned on me, cold and clear, that perhaps my sister had to run away for me to carry on. Because, in a way, it was essential that one of us should leave never to return. It saved both of us the discomfort and the pain of sitting together as adults and talking about everything except those nights on the blue bedspread, that July night on the blue bedspread, moments that were key to our survival and yet better left untouched and unsaid.

On certain rainswept nights, when I lie in bed, I can see Father standing in the rain outside, his hair all wet, the water streaming across his face. He looks half his size, gone is the fat around his waist, the furrows in his forehead. Instead he looks weak, lost, like a child left stranded in the blinding rain.

I want to open the window, ask him to come in, change his clothes and cover him with a blanket. I want to tell him that what happened happened and it's been selfish of me to keep using him as an excuse for failures of my own making. Or as a subject of my prose. I want him to help me understand why he failed as a father and how could so much hatred and pain have gracefully coexisted with so much love and joy.

But when I look at the window again it's too late, Father is gone, leaving behind the rain pouring out from a dark Calcutta night, I can see it streak across the halogen lamps, tap on my window, gurgle around the Municipal Corporation tap.

I close my eyes hard, imagine my wife asleep by my side, my only child awake reading a picture book, or my two children silently conspiring in their bedroom. And I hope that my sister, wherever she is, is safe and has children of her own and when they sleep at night, maybe she sets the stars free once again and their heads come to fit exactly in the curve of her neck.

SUNIL GAVASKAR

Every family has its moments. When the lights in the house dim or brighten, depending on what looks the best, when music begins to play or silence slips in, depending on what sounds the best.

If it's June, a cool wind begins to blow, clouds cover the sun deep within their folds. And if it's January, the sun sets later than usual, your lips don't chap, you can take off your socks, touch the floor with your toes.

People talk in laughs, think in smiles, and for that moment, even if it lasts only one second or one minute, there's happiness spread all around, like chocolates. You can take as much as you want, stuff your pencil box, squeeze some into the hole of your sharpener, even between the pages of your textbooks. And there will be lots left.

Some will stick to the walls, the furniture, some will fall under the bed, in those corners where eyes never reach so that when the moment has passed all you need to do is to search in the right places, keep your ears open for the rustle of the chocolate's wrapping paper, your nails overgrown, so that when you have to chip it off the walls, you can.

This is the story of one such moment.

But because this happened on a September night long ago and because this is December and in a couple of hours it will be day, we will have to twist a few things to get it right. So I will have to tell you to close your eyes; if the wooden slats in the window cannot keep the sun out, you will have to cover your face so that your eyes rest in the dark hollow of your arm.

This should cut the sunlight off, make it easier for you to imagine that it's night, that all the lights have been switched off in this house. Except for one, the table lamp in the room in which I sit, writing.

Because this was Father's room.

Keep your eyes closed and when no one's looking, when you have imagined enough so that the darkness fills the entire room, open your eyes and you can see, at the foot of your bed, a tiny yellow line.

It's very faint, it's coming from Father's room and it takes a distinct shape only when the wind blows and the drapes part. It's then that the line lengthens, even bulges in the middle.

Now, let's get the sound right. Outside, the traffic is thin, once in a while, something passes by, maybe a truck, an empty bus, washed and ready. You can hear the fan tonight but imagine that it's the sound of someone breathing. There may be other noises but let's hope they don't distract. Like a leaf falling, or one of the pigeons in the cage moving in its sleep.

Inside the room, Father is sitting at his table, he hasn't changed his office clothes, the white striped shirt, crumpled, falls below his belt, his trousers are still on, a line of mud crusted on the black fabric, near his ankles. He has unfastened his zip, about one-third, just to relieve the pressure.

But this isn't our focus. For there's nothing unusual. There have been several mornings when he has woken up in his office clothes, sometimes even wearing his watch. Once, he had fallen asleep with his glass, the whiskey stained his bedsheet, the glass broke sometime during the night, under his sleeping weight, a piece cut him near the wrist. He realized it only when he was brushing his teeth and the white washbasin turned red.

Tonight, however, the room smells clean, in all the noises of the night, you cannot make out the clink of glasses, the pouring, the gulps, it's quiet except for the radio.

It's a Philips radio, old, the dust has got into the speaker and the dial so that you can't make out the numbers clearly, the red indicator moves with jerks, the tip of the antenna broke long ago into a stump of steel, jagged at the top. But it serves the purpose as Father chooses short wave, you can hear the click of the knob, he is tuning. The silence breaks.

You can no longer hear the fan in your room, the radio is making a noise, whines, beeps, crackle, some music, crackle again, high-pitched whistles, foreign voices, men and women. As if inside the Philips, there's a huge cinema hall, packed for the matinée show, where men are whistling, clapping, shouting, talking to one another, the pre-show music is on, they are waiting for the lights to be switched off, for the curtains to rise.

Father gets impatient, irritated, he can't get the station, you can hear him curse, get up, push his chair, you close your eyes, afraid, you can hear him fling the curtains aside, the yellow light is now a giant rectangle which touches your bed.

But Father doesn't go to the fridge, doesn't take out any glasses, he goes back to his room, the curtains fall, the radio mutters under its breath, the yellow line has shrunk, your fear melts.

Whine, crackle, whine, crackle, suddenly, no whines, no crackles, absolute silence, Father's got the station, then a soft roar, like when it's raining at night and you are sitting in your room, listening to the rain through a glass window, tightly shut. A man's voice rises from the roar, coming from thousands and thousands of miles away, across the Mediterranean, Central Asia, Iran, across the Arabian Sea, the voice carried by waves heading for the old Philips radio in Father's room.

His hands tremble as the waves enter the speaker, through the dust, and the voice tells him that Bob Willis turns, runs away from us, and the Little Master drives him straight down the wicket, over his head, past mid-off, four more runs, Mike Brearley is worried and Father, who has never played cricket in his life, never watched a cricket match, doesn't need to know what these words mean except that Sunil Gavaskar is nearing his double century, and India, behind by more than one hundred runs in the first innings, can now even win the match, draw the series.

Father can hear the people all the way from the Oval in London, he must have read about the city, seen it in postcards outside the British Airways office, the pigeons at Trafalgar Square, men and women in overcoats, and tonight, India is chasing four hundred and thirty-eight to win, that's all he needs to know as he listens to the runs getting added, one by one, until the voice says that everyone is standing in applause, Gavaskar has scored his two hundred, India cannot lose.

You are lying in bed, and you are listening to the voices, looking at the yellow line on the floor, when the commentators change, Father walks into your room and kisses you on your forehead.

The next morning, it's Teacher's Day, 5 September, we all had to go to school in coloured clothes, classes were off, we had to go early to decorate the classroom, the balloons had to be filled, Teacher's gift had to be wrapped.

'Here, take this,' says Father and he gives us ten rupees each, which means twenty vanilla ice creams, and when we reach school, my sister and I, everyone's talking about how they stayed up last night, burst crackers and how they will, after the Teacher's Day function, go to New Market to buy Gavaskar posters.

And they look at us, brother and sister, and ask us what did you do, we don't say much, we smile and turn away because we can still feel Father's lips on our foreheads, the twenty ice creams waiting, and we know that for the next one week, maybe even two, we will be the happiest children in the city.

Street Crossing

⤞⊜⤝

For once, let me say this. And I promise I shall never say it again tonight: I'm afraid.

This is a story about a man crossing a street.

He may not be a young man, his stomach may droop over the belt of his trousers, but look at him walk to the bus stop every morning and you can make out that he knows his city, so casually he crosses the street.

Others stop, look left, look right, take one step forward, one step back, hold on to their children's hands, tell them, 'Don't hurry, wait for the bus to go.'

He walks straight ahead.

In one sweep of his eyes, without even raising his head, he takes the entire road, its entire traffic from one end to the other. A split second and he's done his arithmetic: the distance he needs to traverse, his speed, by how much does a bus slow down when it approaches a stop, so that he is sure he will make it before the bus does.

Every time, he gets it right.

At the bus stop, he doesn't fidget like the rest. He stands still, calm, the crowd swirls around him like rainwater around a lamp-post.

When a bus pulls up, the others run forward, push each other, crane their necks to see the route number, ask the conductor if it goes where they want to go. But he stands there, looking at something entirely different.

Sometimes the sky or the tram lines. Sometimes, the pigeons in the cage.

He doesn't have to check or ask, he knows when his bus will come. He knows it will wait for him, he will walk towards it, no hurry, no furtive looking at the conductor, he will climb up the steps, if there are many people standing inside, he will walk as if he's the invisible man. No one will tell him, 'Watch your step, mister.'

At work, he doesn't manufacture smiles or frowns, he walks straight to his desk, he can see, sideways, the others gathering in small groups, talking about their buses, their children, mid-term exams, last night's cinema on TV.

He gets down to work.

What does he do? It doesn't matter.

Look at him once again, as he takes out the stapler, the Scotch tape, the Gem clips. He arranges the sheets of paper, flicks the dust off his desk, wipes his typewriter clean with a yellow cloth. Opens his notebook to today's date, his list, neatly written down, of things to do.

Insignificant things but into each he breathes a grand sense of purpose.

Question: Where does this confidence come from?

Answer: Part instinct, part habit, both honed over fifteen years, every day, minus Sundays and holidays. There's another answer: loneliness.

This city likes lonely people, the city likes this man.

There's no one to walk by his side, to wait for him at a street crossing, so the city moves in to help, it slows down the traffic, parts the crowds. There's no one to talk to him, so the city speaks through its banners, its hoardings. At night, he has nothing to do, so the streets tell him their stories, street lights trap insects in their plexiglas covers, lull him to sleep.

No wonder he is so grateful to his city and returns the favour whenever he gets a chance. For example, when buildings, more than a hundred years old, streaked with moss and rain, not worth a second look, tug at his sleeves, he stops in his tracks to watch and admire. Once, twice, even thrice.

On days when the streets are deserted, trade unions have called a strike, he stays up extra hours, gives the city company, listens to its stories like a loyal child.

Until one night his phone rings.

'I am sorry, sir, your sister is dead.' It's the Superintendent of Police, Lake Town, Calcutta 700089. 'She was pregnant . . . We can't keep the body for long . . . the baby is alive, it's a baby girl.'

Now the baby is in the next room, sleeping. The city is outside the window, watching.

During the night, the man gets up to check on the baby, to see why it's silent, why it's crying. He opens the fridge to find out if there's enough milk for the morning, he will prop pillows against the baby, gently close the door so that it doesn't make a noise. And while he is doing all this, the city keeps watching him, irritated and angry.

In just a few hours, the darkest of the night, the foundations of their friendship will crack, the pillars of his solitude, the walls, will begin to buckle, some will even give way. The night will grow darker, the city, once spurned, will begin searching for another lonely man or woman in some other neighbourhood.

And until then, until it finds a new friend, all alone, it will keep coming back to haunt the man, filling him with fears and dreads he has so far never imagined.

Like, how will he cross the street tomorrow morning.

That's why, for once, let me say this. And I promise I shall never say it again tonight: I'm afraid.

MOTHER

WHITE WASHBASIN

Read this once, read this twice, thrice. Come back to it
when you have the time. Read this carefully, then imagine
it, feel it, hear the sounds in it. If you grow up to be a
painter, paint it. Because it's short and fleeting. It's here,
it's not here, it lasts for about two seconds and then it
disappears, like smoke gone with the wind.

It's the only distinct image I can recollect of my
mother, your grandmother. She's standing near a white
washbasin.

There's one more memory, a fragment, more sound
than image: she is waking up in the middle of the night.
Then there's nothing. Except her giant photograph, two
dead cockroaches trapped in its glass frame, in the room
where you sleep.

In my veranda, there's a washbasin, a sink, white
ceramic, your usual washbasin, nothing fancy, just one

steel tap, no faucets like they show in magazines, no hot/
cold knobs marked red for hot, blue for cold, no spark-
ling steel rings attached to drain covers. Just one white
washbasin, stained in a few places, one steel tap, its base
corroded.

It's here that I wash my hands after dinner, brush my
teeth every morning, I have to bend at the waist to turn
the tap on, sometimes it hurts, I am not a young man any
more.

Above the washbasin, there's a wooden shelf, where I
keep my brush, my shaving mug, my razor blades, a
sponge, a bar of soap. There's also a small plastic bird, I
don't know where it came from. It's been lying there for
how many years, I don't know. It's got some soap on it,
dried, marks of water drops that must have splashed up
from the washbasin below.

I am a child, three or four, naked, standing in the washbasin, my head just touches the underside of the shelf so
that I am a near-perfect fit, my feet are on the basin's
floor, my calves touch the tap. Mother holds me at the
waist, it's not winter since I'm not shivering.

It's early morning, through the iron grille of the
veranda, I can see the tram wires, the bus stop across the

street, I can see buses come and go. I can feel the water run in circles around my feet, I hear Mother's glass bangles making a noise as she rubs the soap on my chest. I balance myself, my left hand rests on my mother's head, I can see the red vermilion in the parting of her hair.

And while she is bathing me, suddenly she stops and turns. The soap slips out of her hand, slithers down my body, falls with a thud against the ceramic, my body is half-covered with soap and water. Her head turns, I lose balance, my fingers slide against her hair, my feet press hard against the washbasin, my back rubs against the wall. It's rough, I can feel the white plaster on my skin.

She looks out, across the roof of the shanties, over the tram wires, to the bus stop where a man stands, a tall man with glasses, and she waves to him, she lifts my hand and waves it too, the man waves back, he's smiling, she smiles back, she turns quickly, picks up the soap, the tap is running so the water by now has formed a pool near my legs, she scoops some of it, pours it onto my shoulders.

A bus stops across the street, screens the man, the bus is gone, the man is gone and my mother is back to bathing me. Under her breath, I can hear her sing, I try to recall what happens next and all I see is her giant photograph, two dead cockroaches trapped in its glass frame.

And all I remember is my hand resting on her head, my fingers on the red vermilion in the parting of her hair. And that the man across the street wasn't my father.

SNOW FALL

Mother gets up in the middle of the night, I can remember the sound, the blanket rustling, she moving, her feet touching the floor, she goes to the bathroom and on her way back, after she pulls the flush and the gurgling in the tank dies down, after she switches off the lights, maybe she hears it.

At first, it seems like a medley of several noises. The muted roar from a cricket stadium, the noise of rain falling and then it gets softer. It must be a very light rain, so light that before the drops reach the earth, the wind carries them away, back into the sky. And then it changes, into the sound of something soft rubbing against glass, like when you take a piece of cotton wool and let it slide down the face of a mirror.

By this time she's back in the bedroom, it's dark but it doesn't matter, it's been her bedroom for more than fifteen years, the dressing table is in the same place as it was when she first moved in, so she walks in the dark, glides, without bumping against anything, without making any noise, up to the door which leads into the balcony.

Carefully, so that we don't wake up, so that Father doesn't wake up, she opens the green wooden door, it creaks and she steps out. And it's then that she sees the snow.

White in the dark.

She closes her eyes once and then opens them, she closes her eyes twice, opens them again, nothing has changed. It's white in the dark.

There's no moon tonight and when her eyes adjust she can see the banyan tree across the street covered in white, the flakes falling in the night, catching the light from the street lamps so that it seems a million glow-worms have burst down from the sky.

The snow is there wherever she looks, covering the tram tracks, all the way to where Main Circular Road meets Grey Street, where the flour mill is. The snow covers the film posters on the lamp-posts, she can see the white streaks in the hero's hair, running down the heroine's neck, the snow has covered the little trolley, its lettering, *Amit Egg Rolls*, from which Amit, BA (History Honours), twenty-seven years old, runs his shop.

The snow has entered everything, his gas stove, the place where he keeps the chopped onions and the chillies, the bottle of tomato sauce, the box with the loose change.

At the bus stop, the snow has piled up in three heaps, over the garbage, making them look like old men and women sleeping on a white floor, huddled under white sheets.

To her left, the slums, too, are white, the snow sticks to the TV antennae, the cable wires like glistening cobwebs. The roofs of the shanties across the street are white, the tarpaulins showing in a few tiny patches of blue.

There's no one on the street, all the houses are dark, the windows barred and shuttered, she can't see the pigeons in the cage near the oil mill.

She looks at the sky which is now a huge white sari, the kind which widows wear, spread out over the grass to dry, crinkled in several places, the white fading away into a colour between light ash and deep grey. She feels dizzy, as in the first months of her first pregnancy, she wants to cry out but her lips are dry, she can hear herself breathe, the sound like that of the snow falling.

There's not much of a wind, a few flakes have stuck to the grille in the balcony and before they can melt she touches them, shivers, watches them run down in lines of cold water, over the rusted iron and over her fingers.

She walks back into the bedroom, closes the door, it creaks again, she can see the reassuring shapes of her family in the dark, the two children, under the blanket, on the adjacent bed.

There's work to do before they wake up. So she walks into the dining room where the two Godrej almirahs are, she switches on the lights, pulls the drapes so that the light doesn't reach the bedroom and then she begins to unpack the heavy woollens.

The black coat Father got during his wedding, the leather gloves he hasn't worn for twenty years. For the daughter, she takes out the blue jacket she bought last year from the Tibetan hawkers who sit on Chowringhee Road behind Hind Cinema.

For her son, she takes out the red socks she had bought for herself but doesn't wear, they will be too large for his feet but a little bit of folding will take care of that. And they will reach up to his knees. As for herself, she chooses the Kashmiri shawl Father bought her a month after their wedding.

These woollens will not be enough but there's nothing

she can do. She recalls the household tip she got from a magazine: it's warmer if you wear two thin sweaters rather than one thick one since the air gets trapped in between the layers and prevents the warmth from running away. She can smell the mothballs in the clothes, she can hear the snow still falling in the night.

And in the first light of the next day, when the sun's rays, already weakened by the clouds, enter the bedroom through the green window pane, lighting the edges of the bedsheet, she wakes up her children and her husband and they all go to the balcony.

Other parents and children have come out of their homes, too, the rich ones who have read English books, whose parents have visited foreign countries, who get to watch American shows on Bangladesh TV, know what to do. They build snowmen, tie their old red ribbons around their necks, paint cricket balls black and put these for eyes and ears.

The children of the shanties stay at home, wrapped up in blankets and newspapers. The TV is down, there's nothing to do, they ask their parents what the whiteness is all about and their parents say they don't know. Sometimes, they come out to stand at the door and watch the other children throw snow at one another.

As for us, we are the family in the middle, so we spend the entire day in the balcony. Father in his black wedding coat which goes all the way up to his knees. My sister in her blue coat, my oversized red socks folded near the toes so that I don't trip. Mother, wrapped in the Kashmiri shawl, rests her head against Father's chest, he wraps one arm around her for the first time in my life and Sister and I turn the other way, slightly embarrassed but very happy as Mother reaches out and draws us to her. We can smell the mothballs in her shawl as she tells us the story of how she got up last night and heard the snow, like a piece of cotton wool sliding down the face of a mirror.

She tells us the story for the tenth time but it doesn't matter and we all laugh, Father holds Mother closer to her, my sister puts her hands in mine and we hold on to each other, the air trapped between our clothes, asking all the gods we know not to let the snow melt.

White in the dark.

Sarah Parker

You've been crying for more than five paragraphs.

You began when we stood in the balcony watching the children play with the snow, tying their old red ribbons around their snowmen's necks, painting cricket balls black for the eyes and the ears. The TV was down, there was nothing to do, you cried and you cried.

Don't worry, the police officer had told me. Newborns often cry at night, just like that. It doesn't always mean they need a feed. Let them cry for a while and they usually go back to sleep.

You haven't. What do I do?

Maybe I should hold you in my arms, my left hand below your head, my right arm underneath your back, your ear against my heart, and take you to the balcony. Show you, through the iron grille, the oil mill where the red flags still droop, where the pigeons stand fast asleep. And maybe if we are lucky, we can see some of them, white and grey patches in the night, their heads turned the other way, their beaks buried in their backs.

We could also stand where your mother stood once upon a time and watched one pigeon die. But it's very dark outside and they say that at this time of the year, late November, dewdrops keep falling from the sky. I could cover you with my handkerchief but then there are sodium vapour lamps on the street. Your eyes will hurt.

The nurse at the hospital has given me a pacifier but she said to wait for a couple of weeks, use it when she's strong enough to move her lips. So I shall wait.

I've read in foreign magazines about things that may help you fall asleep. Tapes that play the music of the womb, mattresses that move up and down as if they have your mother's heart inside. But I don't think we get these things in the city.

I could try Toy Centre on Park Street, they say that shop gets its stocks from London, sometimes from Tokyo.

There's some milk in the fridge but it's too cold and by the time I warm it, you may slip into sleep again. I could take you to my study, the room where I'm writing, and put you on the stack of pages that have been written. Maybe the change of place will calm you, from the blue bedspread to the white paper.

But pages flap, their edges are sharp, it's not safe.

If only Miss Sarah Parker were alive, I wouldn't be so helpless. Let me tell you the story of Miss Parker.

Long ago, more than one hundred years ago in fact, there was an American woman who worked out of an office of the Calcutta Municipal Corporation in Chowringhee.

When you grow up and if you live in this city, you will have to go to Chowringhee quite often. That's where all the big offices are, government and private, the markets with fashionable clothes, the pavement vendors who sell eyeglasses in the summer, sweaters in the winter. That's where the big movie halls are, the Everest Building is, the tallest in the city.

Chowringhee is where most of the buses and trams begin and end their journey. It's the heart of the city and like blood, we keep rushing there, through the veins and the arteries of the streets and the lanes. To and fro, to and fro.

So that's where there was a woman called Miss Sarah Parker. And at 7, Chowringhee, she set up a one-room office and she called it the Mesmeric Institute.

Every evening, after office hours, when everyone had

gone, when it was quiet, when you couldn't hear the horses' hoofs any more, in those days they must have had horse-drawn carriages, she called her friends, wrote a Word on a slip of paper, folded it, put it on the table, and asked them to close their eyes.

They all closed their eyes at the same time and when they wanted to open them again, they couldn't. It was as if the eyelids were stuck with glue, they arched their eyebrows, grimaced, blinked and blinked. But nothing. They could not open their eyes until she said the Word.

It must have been a strange sight. There was no electricity then, it must have been in the glare of gaslight or flickering hurricane lamps that she sat in the middle with her subjects all around her, in a semi-circle, all with their eyes closed, their shadows falling on the wall. And outside, the last of the horse carriages going clippety-clop, clippety-clop.

Only when she spoke that Word could they open their eyes.

Then she would ask them to raise their arms and they kept them raised, rigid; they could not bring them down until she said that Word. Sometimes she went even further. Their legs would lose all sensation, they would pinch each other, hit each other on the knees, but feel nothing.

Some of them would even roll off their chairs and

fall on to the floor, some in pain, their legs gone to sleep, but Miss Parker never moved, she sat there, in the centre, looking at them until they were convinced that she had the mesmeric power.

Then she would speak that Word and everything would be normal once again. The sensation would return, her friends would look at her in admiration and fright, at each other with shame and guilt. There would be some nervousness in the air, some tension but all that would disappear in a moment as Miss Parker would laugh and call out for the drinks and the dinner.

'Calcutta is opening its eyes,' *The Statesman* said that time, 'and in a hot climate like this, the power to mentally order people and oblige them to do our will is not to be despised.'

But Miss Parker is dead.

She was followed by a gentleman from Paris. He called himself a thought reader and he performed at the Dalhousie Institute, a man called Dr Chapagnon.

He's dead, too.

And where Miss Parker once lived, where her house once was, there is today a vegetable market. Janbazar, behind Elite Cinema.

On nights when I return home late and there is no public transport, I go to Janbazar to take a taxi. I stand near the mound of dead vegetable peels, some green but most beginning to rot, and I can hear the noises of the night show in Elite, the shuffle of feet during the interval, the sound of the ice-cream boys shouting at tired customers, the crinkle of potato chips being eaten in the night.

If Miss Parker were alive tonight, I promise I would have gone to get her. The writing would have waited. I would have got a taxi, paid the driver extra since it's so late, asked him to take me to the Mesmeric Institute at 7, Chowringhee.

I would have woken her up and if she or her servant had refused to open the door, I would have stood on the street and shouted, 'Miss Parker, Miss Parker, wake up, wake up,' I would have asked her, begged her, gone down on my knees, on the street, so what if the tar tore the fabric of my trousers, I would have forced her to come with me, to step into the waiting taxi, I would have brought her to your room and asked her to write the Word, make you sleep, make you stop crying so that you wake up only when she says the Word in the morning.

But that's not to be.

*

So I go back to my pages, I begin to finish the story about the night snow fell in our neighbourhood, how Mother reached out and drew us close, under her shawl, we could smell the mothballs as she told us the story of how she got up that night and heard the snow, like a piece of cotton wool sliding down a mirror, I can hear you crying.

But I write, word after word, and as each sentence comes to life, grows up and dies, your crying gets softer and softer, it seems someone is taking you away from me, walking into the distance, so that by the time I finish the story, it's all over, you've gone back to sleep, leaving behind your crying ringing in my ears like a faraway bell.

SISTER

DEAD PIGEON

(A story in two parts)

They found him in the morning, five thirty or so, hanging from a hook on the bedroom ceiling where his fan should have been. His walking stick was on the floor, the chair he had climbed on lay upturned, its four legs marking a rectangle in which his body swung gently, like that of a lamb, upside down, at a butcher's shop.

The police came around seven, in a red and white jeep; a red light on the roof which didn't work; a constable got up on the chair, held him tight with one hand, loosened the blue nylon rope with the other, lowered him down.

'He's very light,' he said. 'He's so old he would have died anyway, why did he have to kill himself?' he said.

Why did he have to kill himself?

The constable took this question and walked around the neighbourhood, to as many people as he could, but no one had the answer. No one knew where the old man came from, whether he had any relatives in some faraway

99

village. Or whether there were some people in the city who would cry themselves to sleep that night.

So they followed the rules, as laid out in the book, typed out a notice at the police station which no one came to read. And, therefore, forty-eight hours later, they cremated him.

He was seventy, they said, no medical college needed a cadaver so old. He could even have been eighty, it didn't matter.

It was one of the four suicides in the city that day; it would become, by the end of the month, one of a hundred and fifty. By the end of that year, one of over fifteen hundred. Multiply that by fifteen for fifteen years and what do you have left?

Nothing, the old man is gone.

Gone also is his house, it wasn't a house exactly, just a four-wall shack, with a tarpaulin roof, beside the road, which they demolished the day after they found him. There was nothing in the room except an extra walking stick, an iron chair, clothes that smelled of his years and some pigeon feathers scattered below the bed, some underneath his pillow.

They took it all away, leaving behind nothing to mark the fact that once upon a time there lived an old man. And that for a week or so, he changed the life of a little *girl, brought joy into her house and filled her little heart with some love.*

Once upon a time, there lived an old man who worked in an oil-refining mill, pasting labels on tin cans, just before the oil was poured into them: bright yellow labels with pictures of Lord Ganesh, in black and red, the name of the mill in blue: Ganesh Oil Mill, Calcutta 700006.

How long he'd been doing this, no one knows, but it must have been quite a while because if you looked carefully you could see that his fingers were crinkled as if glue had dried on them and merged with his skin.

When he picked up a piece of paper, any piece of paper, through instinct and habit he made it look as if he were holding a label, he held it gingerly, between the thumb and his finger, looking all around him as if he were lost, as if he were searching for a place to paste it, somewhere, anywhere.

Just outside the oil mill, a couple of feet to the right of its entrance, were the birds. In a large cage, more like a coop, the kind you will see at the Alipore Zoo, slightly smaller, the size of an average storeroom in an average house. Three sides of the cage were walls, the fourth that faced the road was strong wire netting.

There were twelve pigeons in the cage, six grey, six

white, the prettiest things in the neighbourhood. And although there were several pigeons out in the open, resting on window ledges, cooing in the afternoon, fluttering in the narrow lanes and doing pretty things like scratching their backs or sleeping, people stopped by to look at these dozen birds in the cage.

Flying round and round, grey and white, grey and white. On certain rainy days, when the sky was dark, it seemed tiny clouds had slipped into the cage each dragging with it just a little bit of the sky. And then one afternoon in 1977, the oil mill closed down. Just like that, all of a sudden.

It was the time they started painting Moral Science lessons on trucks and trams, buses and taxis. In black cursive letters:

Work more, talk less. Honesty is the best policy.

The owner of the oil mill, a heavy man in a silk kurta and dhoti, his chin glowing from the necklaces around his neck, there were at least four, drove up to the mill door that evening, stepped out of his car, and walked to the gate, two locks, one in each hand. The workers waved red flags, shouted their protests, one even spat in his direction but it didn't matter because the owner kept walking as if he couldn't hear; with a smile on his face, he locked the gates, put the keys in his pocket, the workers heard the clink and he began to walk back to his white Ambassador. When suddenly, he stopped.

He saw the old man in the crowd and he walked up to him, the old man, afraid, hid behind some young men, the owner put one hand on his shoulder, lowered his mouth to his ear and said something which made the old man smile. This whole thing lasted not more than fifteen seconds before he turned and walked away towards the car.

Some workers, the more angry ones, ran after the car, chased it over a distance but the car was faster. They returned, cursing the man, calling him names, they then circled the old man, asked him what the owner had said.

One young worker shouted at him. 'Don't double-cross us,' he said. 'Don't stab us in the back,' another said.

The old man just smiled, a sad and nervous smile, and said, no, there was no deal, the owner had told him to take care of the pigeons, to look after them, to see to it that they got fed every day and the cage was cleaned every morning.

This gave the workers some hope because it showed that the owner had a little bit of his heart still left. And no one protested, no one was against the pigeons.

But like water in the sun, this hope began to disappear, in patches, so that by the time summer slipped into the monsoons, it was gone. A team from the Labour Commissioner's office came to inspect but nothing happened, the mill never opened.

Some workers stayed there at the entrance, shouting slogans, propped up their flags against the door, and when it was too late, when the rest of the neighbourhood had gone to sleep, they sat down, in a bunch, played cards until they fell asleep.

As the rains came, the flags got drenched, discoloured, the red turned into some pale brown, the older workers began to leave the group, in ones and twos, to look for other jobs. The younger ones waited and waited to teach the owner a lesson but nothing happened. Until one day, they too went away, leaving behind the red flags drooping over the signboard. Only two things remained unchanged and unaffected: the pigeons and the old man.

From the very first day, they fell in love, the old man and the birds.

Morning, afternoon, evening, he sat on an iron chair,

his back to the road, as if in a painting, looking at the birds. When it rained, he sat with an umbrella; when it got cold, he sat with a shawl draped over his head, a small pile of wood, old newspapers, burning at his feet.

Exactly at eight every morning, when the siren from the flour mill, about half a kilometre away, went off, he would get up, steady himself with the walking stick and climb up the two steps that led to the door of the cage. He would unlock it, enter the cage, close the door behind him, pick up the broom that lay on the floor.

The birds flew around him, some perched on his shoulder, on his back, their feathers falling across his face but the old man looked as if he were walking in paradise, in the snow, all wrapped up and warm, the flakes falling across his face.

Until one day, when he walked inside, something happened, maybe a wind blew or there was something wrong with the hinges since the door, which he had pushed close, opened, not much, just a tiny crack restoring the link between the cage and the outside world, enough for one white pigeon to fly away.

Now pigeons aren't great fliers to begin with and this one was perhaps a young one since it fluttered for a while, hopped and then flew, only to go and sit on the tram wire above the street, looking this way and that, unsure what to do with its sudden freedom.

The old man hurried out, half-stumbling, half-walking, locked the door, stood at the edge of the pavement, called out loud to the bird. It didn't listen, he picked up a stone, threw it, it didn't travel far, his hands were weak, he beat his walking stick on the iron chair, the noise was loud but the pigeon just turned its head to scratch its back.

It continued to sit, its feet glued to the wire, it looked around, at the banyan tree near the oil mill, at the cage, it rubbed its beak against its neck, it preened itself. Not once did its little feet feel the tingle of the No. 12 tram from Esplanade to Galiff Street which was now just a couple of feet away.

By now, the old man was hysterical. He called out to the tram driver; someone was walking by, he stopped her, asked her to call the driver, she walked by. 'Fly away,' the old man shouted, 'fly away,' but it was as if the bird was made of stone.

The tram clanged, the old man shouted, the woman who walked by stopped and she shouted too, a crow, like an accidental ally, joined them, fluttered over the pigeon but nothing helped. The tram moved, the old man saw the pigeon fall, the white bundle drop onto the roof of the tram and then slide down, along the side, the dead pigeon, its tiny feet up in the air, its head lolled to one side.

He rushed to pick up the bird but before he could step off the pavement a double-decker bus, No. 11A bound for Howrah Station, came rushing by, followed by a couple of taxis, another bus, a truck, so that by the time the road had cleared, most of the dead bird was gone leaving a reddish-brown stain on the manhole cover, some feathers drenched with blood.

And as the day wore on, as vehicles kept going up and down the street, moving across the dead bird, parts of it stuck to the tyres, big and small, slow and speeding, so that by the end of the day, bits and pieces of the bird travelled across the city.

The old man went back to his iron chair, one white bird less, the cage looked darker. Whether the old man cried we don't know. Even if he had, no one would have noticed since it was about nine o'clock, time to go to office, time to go to school. Except for a little girl, about ten or twelve years old, standing in the balcony of her house, across the street from the oil mill, a little girl who saw everything and began to cry.

The old man turned to sit down in his chair, this time

facing the road, his back towards the cage, and when he turned, he saw this girl, dressed in her white nightdress, with red flowers all over.

He couldn't see her eyes, he was at quite a distance, but the sight of the girl, standing in the balcony, looking at him with a face wet with what could only be tears, offered him not only a distraction from his sadness but also a chance to silently share his loss, if only for a moment.

Our story will, after a while, move across the street, over the manhole, over the reddish-brown stain, into the girl's house and from there, into her heart, in one straight line.

NIGHT GAME

On winter nights, just before Father switched off the lights in our bedroom, your mother and I played the Blanket Game.

Our eyes still open, we pull the blanket over our heads, stretch it tight, turn over on our sides so that we face each other. And then we look at the light refracted through the woollen fabric. It's a blue yellow orange red light, a strange glow that you see only in the movies.

We then imagine that we have built our own light garden, its floor the blue bedspread, its roof the blanket and its flowers the red flowers on my sister's white nightdress, the checks and stripes on my shirt.

There are several smells in our garden. The earth is the blanket, musty and warm; the grass is our clothes, smelling of water and soap and sun, the blue bedspread is the night, the flowers are my sister's shampoo, the wind is the breath of approaching sleep.

But soon it becomes difficult to breathe, so we raise one end of the blanket, the one over our head, let the cold, fresh air rush in and then we dive underneath, back to our garden.

Sometimes we feel bold, so we hold the blanket high. We balance it, adjust it with our hands, so that the tassels on its fringe hang straight down, touch the blue bedspread in such a way that they seem like pickets for the fence of our light garden.

Then the light streams in, it gets brighter, it's daytime in our garden, the colours of the flowers change. Until Father switches off the light and our garden melts into the night, the flowers go to sleep.

We played this game for quite a few winters until we found that we were growing bigger and bigger, the blanket, after we were covered, couldn't reach far enough to be held high and tight, the garden then grew smaller and smaller.

But I needed to tell you this little story, my child, so that when you have to pull your blanket over your head, remember that with a little bit of imagination, you can always find some love trapped in some fear.

Durga Puja

Mike testing, ten, nine, eight, seven six five, four three two onezero. Testing, mike testing, ten, nine, eight, it's the first day of the Pujas and she is ironing their clothes, his mother has to go for the prayer later in the day, she can see the thin man climb up the lamp-post, another holding the ladder, he adjusts the microphone underneath, the huge black and yellow banner for Boroline, the antiseptic cream for all seasons.

There are neat circular holes punched in the banner. Grandfather told her, long ago, those holes are for the wind to pass through so that the banner doesn't tear.

She still cannot understand why. Maybe it has to do with forces acting on a rectangular surface, her school physics. Wherever she goes, she finds these banners, calling out to her across the city, strung across two lamp-posts on either side of the street, above the tram wires. Sometimes even across two houses in narrow lanes. All kinds of banners. Sure Success Tutorials for the Joint

Entrance Examinations, Slimline Beauty Clinic, Complete Course in Computer Programming.

But this black and yellow Boroline banner comes up only during the Pujas, around the pandals, the huge tents made of canvas and cane, set up in the neighbourhood to welcome the Goddess who comes down from the hills, with her children, to her father's place. For ten days every year.

Since last year, they also have a blue and white banner as big as Boroline's, but this one's for Fair and Lovely, the cream which dissolves the brown and keeps the skin fair and glowing. She'd bought it once, Mother threw it out, 'You are dark and you are beautiful,' she had said.

She bought one again after her marriage, used it every day, she bought it twice, thrice until her husband said, 'Forget it, let's wait for something better.'

His shirt and trousers are done, she has draped them over the dining-table chair, he will go with his mother to the pandal; his mother's blouse has been ironed, the sari is left.

She remembers the candy man in Deoghar where she went for the Pujas long, long ago, the old man with the long bamboo pole against his shoulder, the candy wrapped around at the top, a big red and white ball. Twenty paise and he lowered the pole, tore off a chunk and asked her what shape would she like it in.

She always preferred the watch, so he tore a chunk off the candy ball and made a watch for her, the dial is white, the straps are red that go over her wrists. 'They go well with your dress, little girl,' he said.

Grandfather always paid him extra, told him, 'Buy something for your children, they must be waiting for you at home.' And she would feel the heavy candy on her wrist, watch the candy man walk away.

She liked to lick the straps first and then the dial, the dial was sweeter. 'Wash your wrists with soap after you are done,' Mother said. 'Otherwise, ants will come at night.'

She can hear him in the bathroom, pouring the water over his body, mugs and mugs, she can hear the silences in between as he soaps himself. She removes a hanger from the wardrobe for his mother's ironed blouse, hangs it from the hook on the wall, above the Tata Steel calendar.

It shows October, the month of nuts and bolts, magnified in black and grey, about twenty-five times, so that the threads on the screws are visible, like whorls on some iron fingers. The calendar page flaps gently in the wind but the ironed blouse firmly keeps it in place.

Mike testing. Eight-year-old Anshuman has come from Barasat, he is with us at the Puja Organizing Committee office, his mother, please come and pick him up. Anshuman, eight years old, is from Barasat. He is sitting here, right in front of us, please come and pick him up. This is a message to all parents, please take care of your children, tell them to hold your hand, we will do our best.

His father sits on the sofa, his legs up, reading *The Statesman*, the only newspaper that's printing in the Pujas. They have a picture of the Goddess on the front page, a Goddess with dark lipstick, high cheekbones and a blouse that glitters.

Through the window she can see the house across the slums, the Saha household, the father works with Indian Airlines, he gets packets of fresheners for his children, sometimes even unopened breakfast and lunch boxes, complete with the little plastic packet which has the silverware, knives and forks, one big spoon for the rice, one tiny spoon for the dessert. And one toothpick per lunch.

Saha has two children, a brother and a sister, and today she can see them in their balcony, the sister in a new Puja yellow and red dress, resting her face against the grille. She had done the same thing once and Father had said, 'Don't sit like this, the iron will leave marks on your face, spoil your skin.'

She spreads the sari across the iron board, the ends fall against the floor.

'Careful, now,' says his mother from the next room. She bends, picks up the ends of the sari.

'Be careful, not so hot, it's silk,' says his mother.

And she begins ironing the sari, bit by bit, the sweat rolling down her neck into her blouse, onto her breasts. She shivers, watches her wrist, the candy that's not there. He's out of the bathroom now, drying himself, she can hear the towel rustle against his body, her husband's body, his hair.

'Hurry up,' says his mother. 'His trousers should be ready, he shouldn't catch a cold. The weather is changing.'

*

She can hear the mike again. *We are pleased to inform you that Anshuman's parents have found him, please take care of your children.*

Mike testing, the counting begins again, ten nine eight, the wind rushes, suddenly, from nowhere, through the holes in the banners, some of it enters the room, fans her face, and for some strange reason she begins to cry, seven six five, the tears fall on his mother's sari and she presses the hot iron, four three two, steams the drops away. One, zero, she's ready.

MATERNITY WARD

The glass window is large, the drapes are grey and heavy but she's pushed them aside, there was a bit of a problem since one of the hooks, the little white plastic hooks that move along the curtain rod, got stuck.

She tugged, tugged harder, one hook gave way, snapped. It fell to the marble floor. She turned, looked around, just in case someone was watching, but there was no one, who knows whether this is damage to hospital property. But the damage helped, one hook gone, the drapes glided to the left.

Through the window now, she can see the buses and the taxis glide down Shakespeare Sarani, their tail-lights blinking as they turn left at the Ballygunge Circle before disappearing into the dark clouds of their exhaust.

In the little patch of green, between the Maternity

Ward and the Administrative Block, she watches a man and a child, a little girl wobbling on a red bicycle. Their voices float upwards, towards her, but she can't make out what they're saying; the little girl loses balance and the man, perhaps her father, lurches forward to steady the bicycle.

He holds the handlebars with one hand as the little girl, who's wearing a blue frock, adjusts herself. And with his other hand, he holds the seat at the back, half-running, half-walking. Sometimes, his entire body shuts the bicycle out of her view and all she can see then is a middle-aged man running in the garden, half-bent and laughing.

It's evening; not yet seven since they haven't switched on the street lights yet, she likes it this way. Her room is filled with the day's falling light, the white walls dappled red; her wristwatch, kept on the bedside table, has stopped at two thirty.

She will wait for the nurse to tell her the time.

She walks back to her bed, smoothens out the sheets, fluffs the two pillows, puts one on top of the other. She can never get it right at home, he always complains, the pillows break into lumps.

But here, the sheets and the pillows all are white, taut.

He left his red handkerchief when he came to visit her this morning and she spreads it over the pillow. It's crumpled but it looks nice, the tiny rectangle of red, alive on the deathly white of the bed.

She feels tempted to switch on the reading lamp but checks herself: there's nothing to read except some sales literature on the side table, blue and white, on some antacid which sounds vaguely familiar. More than reading, however, she wants to see what the room looks like when the street lights come on, the huge sodium vapour lamps, two in the park, one just outside her window, several lining the street.

Last night, when she woke up for a glass of water, she saw it: a soft yellow glow that made the cold steel bedposts glint softly like gold, warm and rich. The light broke across her window, staining the glass in several colours, like the tall windows of her school church.

And while falling asleep again, as her eyes began to close she began to see scenes of her childhood, half-remembered, half-forgotten: the Monday morning assembly in the St Paul's Church, Sister Lucy reading from the school diary, *God, make me a channel of your peace, an instrument of your love*; the black rubber bands that held her white socks in place.

*

Perhaps there's a traffic jam.

From outside, she can faintly hear the car horns, the revving up of an engine, a man's voice calling out loud. Someone coughs in the hallway: it's the sweeper doing the rounds, and after a while, when the road falls silent, she can hear the sound of his mop scrubbing the marble floor, the slap of his slippers.

She turns back and walks to the window again. This time, the cars are stuck, like brightly coloured ants waiting in line; two police constables are waving their arms. The man and the girl are gone, a rag-picker sits on the yellow bench wrapped in his shadow. She can see that a wind has begun to blow, rustling the leaves of the giant eucalyptus trees in the hospital compound. There's a banner strung between two, with a lot of lettering, from this distance, she cannot make out what's written, maybe she needs glasses.

She can't feel the wind, it's better this way, for through the thin hospital gown she can feel the cold of the room beginning to rub against her skin. The gown is at least one size over: its hem scrapes the floor and she has to be careful lest she trip; the straps keep sliding over her shoulders. The first two days she was too sick to notice; later, she felt uncomfortable, self-conscious; she had asked one of the nurses to change the gown but no, all gowns in the hospital were of a standard size, the nurse said. But now she's got used to it.

And who will stand on Shakespeare Street and stare at a patient looking through the window of a sixth-floor hospital room?

Silly, stupid of me, she thinks, as she returns to lie down on the bed. Her head hits the bedpost hard, she winces. She adjusts the pillows, settles down, pulls the white blanket over her, the head hurts. She turns on her side, she can smell him in the red handkerchief: his aftershave and the sweat, his hands, the thick nape of his neck.

The last time, the only other time she was in a hospital was at her grandfather's place in Deoghar which she visited every Durga Puja. Must have been very long ago because the baby brother hadn't come into the family yet, she can remember the night before.

The train will leave Sealdah station at five thirty in the morning, she goes to bed late, there are a thousand things that have to be done: the picture books have to be shoved deep down in the bag, one has to be kept in Mother's handbag just in case she wants to read in the train; her favourite lipstick is smuggled in along with Mother's bangles and earrings. She can't sleep, it's already two, she has to get up at four since the toothbrush and her nightdress have to be packed too. She keeps staring at the clock on the wall, the chiming magnified in the stillness of the night. From the next room, she can hear her parents discussing which rooms to lock, who should keep the key and where to put the instructions for the maid who has to air the rooms every third day, collect the mail.

When she wakes up, it's pitch dark in the bedroom, she can see the suitcases and the holdall lying on the floor, all ready, packed, huddled like old men and women, waiting to be taken down to the taxi.

Mother has laid out the Train Dress for her on the bed: a black skirt and a red top, dark colours because the dust, the coal from the engine won't show, she says. As she brushes her teeth standing in the veranda that leads to the kitchen, she can hear the clink of tiffin boxes, Mother packing lunch for the journey. Through the iron grille, she can see Father standing at the bus stop looking for a taxi.

Grandfather smells like morning tea; she can smell the soap and the water in his starched shirtsleeves, clean and fresh; his fingers are soft, wrinkled, she holds on to them and walks. The wind fills her skirt, squeezes into her shirt, her eyes. She's the girl from the city and villagers turn their heads to look at her, at her shoes, her hair, black and beautiful, cropped up close, like a boy's.

'We are going to Haathi Pahar,' Grandfather says, 'Elephants' Mount, the British called it. Five huge rocks that look like elephants fast asleep. There's also a tap there, right between the rocks, and for twenty-four hours a day, three hundred and sixty-five days a year, rain or drought, cold or hot, the water keeps flowing, crystal clear. No one knows where the water comes from since there is no stream nearby, no river and as you know, I told you before, this is an arid plateau. Take this flask, we'll fill it up there.'

There's a knock at the door and the nurse walks in, she can hear her walk up to the bed, stand there. It must be a new nurse since she hasn't heard this sound before, the heavy footsteps, the clink of bangles.

'When do you want dinner today, Didi?' the nurse asks.

She pretends she's asleep, tense; the nurse walks to the bedside table, she can hear her move the chair but let the drapes stay where they are.

'When do you want dinner, Didi?' the nurse asks again.

She doesn't move, the nurse clicks her tongue, stands there, fidgets, shuffles her feet and then walks out, closing the door behind her.

She relaxes, the nurse didn't notice the white hook on the floor, she turns on her side, they have switched the street lights on.

From the bed she can see the purple rectangle of night in her window, fringed by the scattered glow from the sodium vapour lamp. She removes the blanket, her gown rides above her knees, slips over her shoulders leaving them bare, she doesn't bother.

They walk past the cluster of tea stalls, smell the milk and the basil leaves boiling, past the rickshaw stand where she notices the rickshaw-puller who brought them from the station, he smiles at her, Grandfather keeps looking straight ahead as they turn left from the metalled road onto the dirt track lined with wild flowers, red and white.

'How far is it, Grandfather?'

'We are almost there,' he says, his face glowing in the morning light, his rimless glasses catching the sun in two bright spots.

And then, suddenly, as soon as they turn the bend, she

can see the rocks, elephants sleeping with their heads buried in the ground. Huge black-grey stones, speckled and warm. Five of them, all roughly the same size, two together, the rest spread out. Like the African herd from her geography textbook, without the heads and the tusks. Two children, about her age, play on one elephant's back.

She lets go of Grandfather's finger, the earth rushes to meet her as she runs, clambers atop one of the rocks.

'Careful, watch your step, look to your right, you can see the temple.'

She looks at the spire built more than three hundred years ago, she can see the big bunch of red ribbons tied around its top, like a red knot on a doll's head. One ribbon tied by each pilgrim for each wish fulfilled.

'Wish,' says Grandfather, 'stand on the rock, look at the spire, close your eyes and wish. Don't say it aloud, just whisper it to yourself so that no one can hear.'

What will she wish for? The red bicycle she saw in the shop window in the central market, the one with a reflecting lamp, handlebars with bright red leather strips and a blue basket in front. 'Where will you ride a bicycle in Calcutta?' Father had said, and she had understood.

But she wishes anyway, for the red bicycle she saw in the shop window.

*

As she turns to climb down, she slips and falls down the rock, her head strikes the rock, her feet drag along the elephant's back, she screams, crashes against the tap, the cold water gurgles over her grazed knee.

Grandfather is there, his black shawl hovering over her like a protective blanket, shutting off the sun from her eyes as he bends down, picks her up. She's conscious but she can't open her eyes, the pain like a flame hissing all over her body, she clutches at Grandfather's shirt, she can smell the starch and her blood, warm across her face, entering her nose, her lips.

Two hours later, she wakes up to the smell of Dettol and incense sticks in a tiny room with Grandfather by her side, holding her hand, Mother at her feet, her eyes closed, her lips moving in prayer.

'Don't worry, you will be all right tomorrow,' Mother says, 'they have stitched your knee up, no bones broken but let's wait for the X-ray so that we know for sure.'

And as she is saying all this, Grandfather motions to someone standing outside the door and in comes the bicycle with the reflecting lamp, the handlebars with red leather strips and the blue basket in front.

'Your wish,' says Grandfather, and although it hurts,

although the white bandage around her head is so tight she can hardly move her eyes, she smiles.

Mother stops praying and the boy who's wheeled the bicycle in begins to jump up and down as if the bicycle were his, begins to ring its bell until the doctor's attendant comes running in and tells them there are other patients too and that this is a hospital, not a market.

Through the gown, she feels her right knee, the stitch marks are still there; so is the scar on her forehead, just above her eyes, half-covered by her eyebrows. He had asked her about it the first night they lay together in bed, naked. She felt his heart, his chin on her head, his huge hands running through her hair.

'Let's get the scar on the forehead removed,' he said. 'Doesn't look nice. Why don't you paint your eyebrows thicker so that it can't be seen?'

She did not reply. 'I am just joking,' he said.

She couldn't sleep, got up for a glass of water, saw the leftovers lying uncovered. Cockroaches darted across the dining table, one floated in the vinegar of the salad, the rice had gone hard. She covered the rice, emptied the vinegar into the sink and returned to bed but she couldn't sleep.

She watched his bare haunches, his arms, his broad

shoulders, the rise and fall of his chest. She kept staring at the fan, trying to count the blades on her first night, the beginning of a lifetime in a two-room flat where the sky squeezes itself into narrow lanes to keep the buildings from touching each other.

That night she dreamt of pregnant women, young and old, their white gowns billowing in the night, dancing in the sky. They hold hands like the skydivers she has seen on TV, they spread their legs and in a sudden gust of wind they give birth. Babies rain, some snap their umbilical cords and break free, others dangle from their mothers' wombs, swaying in the wind. She sees her brother, he's standing in the veranda, waving at her, she looks away, she can see in the sky a blue bedspread flying, she feels the bile rise in her throat, two arms rise up from within her stomach and clutch at her heart.

'Wake up, Didi,' says the nurse.

At first, through the haze of her drowsiness, she doesn't hear. 'Wake up,' the nurse repeats, this time her hand on her shoulder.

'Yes.' That's all she can say as she sees the nurse's face hovering over hers: the grey streaks in her hair, the red plastic earrings, the mole below her lower lip.

'Aren't you hungry? I came in twice before but you didn't wake up.'

The nurse steps back from the bed, walks backwards to stand almost in the centre of the room, half-covering the window.

To her left is the dinner trolley, two steel plates covered with aluminium foil; the door is slightly ajar, light from the hallway enters the room in a narrow white rectangle.

'What time is it?' she asks, her head still hurts, the taste of unfinished sleep in her mouth.

'It's around midnight. I have set your watch right,' she says placing the dinner plate on the bedside table.

Then she walks up to the door as if to leave but she doesn't; she closes the door and stands there. 'I'm not leaving the room until you finish dinner.'

The foil is hot, her fingers recoil, the nurse walks over and peels it off the rim of the plate.

She feels uncomfortable, a stranger watching her eat, her gown slipping off her shoulders. And yet she doesn't want the nurse to go; she stabs at the rice with the spoon. Dinner over, the nurse begins clearing the table.

'I have to hurry,' she says, 'I have already overstayed by two hours. And the last bus leaves at twelve thirty.'

'Where do you live?'

'Barasat, Didi. It takes more than an hour to reach there. At this time, there's no traffic: it will take no more than forty, forty-five minutes.'

'Doesn't your husband complain?'

'What husband? I left him long ago.'

For a moment, she feels uncomfortable: at the unexpected, personal turn the conversation has taken. She feels awkward trying to look for another subject but the nurse doesn't seem to mind as she wipes the table, crumples the aluminium foil, dumps it into the plate, leaves it outside in the hallway.

She returns and helps her with the blanket, adjusts the pillows.

And then, all of a sudden, the nurse removes one of the safety pins that straddle across her bangles and gently fixes the straps of her gown. It's a gesture without any apparent effort and although she knows that the nurse, in all likelihood, is doing her job, the touch of her hands and the way she clasps the pin over the excess fabric makes her feel somewhat safe.

'Now it won't slip off,' she says closing the door behind her. 'Sleep well, Didi. I'll see you tomorrow.'

She can hear her footsteps echo in the hallway, the

sound of the trolley being wheeled back to the kitchen or wherever it came from.

And like the darkness in her room which flows out of the window and merges with the darkness of the city, she can feel, for the first time since her miscarriage, long before you ever came, that she is not alone.

MURDER MYSTERY

'That's the hospital, over there,' he points out.

He points to a strip of white, far away, over her head and her shoulders, across the trees, the clusters of houses, to the left of the plume of grey smoke rising in the sky from some roof, to the right of the white marble dome of the Victoria Memorial.

'That's the hospital where you were stuck for two weeks,' he says. 'And that's Park Street, can't you see the lights?'

Yes, she can, but tonight is his night to show and hers to see and she doesn't want to spoil anything.

Two days to go for 14 April, the Bengali New Year, it's time for the nor'westers, they are standing on the terrace of the new flat they've moved in to and she can feel the wind, the end of her sari clap gently against her leg.

She looks around, at the two huge black water tanks, a piece of wire strung across the TV antennae. There's a clothes clip dangling on the wire but there are no clothes to dry. In one corner, she can see a broken white ceramic toilet bowl, stained, its cover surprisingly shining, black. As if it were new.

They never come up to the terrace although the landlord was sweet the first day they moved in, one week ago, after her miscarriage. His mother and father had said, 'Why don't you people spend some time together, we will come later.'

'You can use the terrace whenever you want. During March and April, it's very nice there,' the landlord had said. 'Colder than your house, you should take a scarf if it's too late.'

'It's a bit dirty but you are young people,' the landlord's wife had said. 'You can do it up, put some flower pots, get the mess cleaned up. We are too old.'

She had smiled at the landlord's wife as she pressed her hand into hers, looked at her husband as he read the rent papers. She could see the veins in his hand as he signed his name.

'Come here, this way,' he says and she follows him, like a child, looking at his white striped shirt and grey trousers, which she ironed twice this morning since he said the crease didn't fall in a straight line, she can see the peak of his white socks, the lights on Park Street, the big white one is the Continental Hotel where they change the mannequins every week.

The line of small red ones, the twinkling lights, must be the Chinese restaurant where they have a picture of a huge dragon on the wall, the menu painted on its tongue. She can see the Calcutta Electric Supply Corporation, its huge lighted globe spinning round and round in circles, Africa is facing her now.

His hands are on the railing and he's looking in the distance, his shirt stretched tight across his back, marking his shoulder blades. He yawns once and rubs his eyes, she knows he will now ask her for a drink.

'Will you get me a drink from downstairs?' he says and she says yes, goes down the steps, she can feel her hands rub against the wall, it's much warmer here, she enters the house, it's dark, she switches the lights on and then she walks into the kitchen.

She picks out two ice cubes from the deep freeze, puts them into a steel glass, she can see her name engraved on it.

She remembers the old man who came every afternoon into the neighbourhood, stopped for a while to look at the pigeons in the oil mill, and then shouted something she then couldn't make out.

One day Mother called him upstairs, gave him her

small steel glass. 'The little girl wants her name on her glass,' he said and still smiling, he patted her on the head.

She watched him take a little hammer out of a small leather bag and a steel pen. He then sat down on the floor, spread his legs and held her little glass between his two feet, his toe leaving giant smudges on the rim. But she didn't mind as he hammered the steel pen, dot after dot, and she saw her name appear on the steel, letter by letter. The job done, he wiped the glass against his trousers. 'Go get two rupees from your mother,' he said.

She pours the drink into the glass, she can hear the crackle as it hits the ice. She walks up the stairs again, this time looking at her shadow riding up the wall, the cold makes her shiver. It will be better now, she thinks as she reaches the terrace landing, his mother is not here, fewer clothes have to be ironed.

When she steps onto the terrace, he's standing near the edge now pointing to a red-brick building, she can see only its top floor and that too just a part of the top floor, a long corridor, lit by one tube light, with several doors, all locked. It reminds her of books, in line on library shelves. The tubelight flickers.

'Can you see that red building?' he says, taking the

drink and then, sipping it, he makes a noise. 'That's my school,' he says.

'It's very difficult to get admissions there now. I went there last week and met the Principal,' he says, still looking at the red building. 'I am a former student so they treated me as a special case. I told them I wanted my child admitted there.'

His drink is almost over, he passes her the glass and she holds it not knowing whether she can go now. She turns back to head for the stairs, she can feel the cold of the steel in her hands, one ice cube is still there, unmelted.

'Where do you think you are going?' he says. 'Didn't you hear what I said, that's where I wanted to send my child. And now what do I tell the Principal?'

She smiles at him, she can feel the wind in her sari again. She looks over his shoulder, away from the school he's pointing to, to another terrace of another house down the street. She can see a woman hanging clothes out to dry, she hears them flap, so late in the night it's surprising, a child looks at the woman and then plays with what looks, from this distance, like a red cricket ball.

'Get me another drink,' he says. 'That's the least you can do.'

'Yes,' she says and she turns.

*

How should we end this story? We could have her go down to get him the second drink, hear the crackle as it hits the ice in the steel glass, climb the stairs again and listen to him talk about the school, the child she couldn't give him.

Or we could end it like this:

She returns with the drink, he doesn't even hear her footsteps, he's looking out, far away, at the lights on Park Street and she walks closer towards him, the glass in her hand. She bends down, puts the glass on the terrace, she will need both hands, his back is turned, the first drink must have blunted his senses since he can't hear or feel that she is only two feet away.

Suddenly there is a scream which no one will hear, a body, dressed in a white shirt and grey trousers, white socks and black shoes, falls into the lane which not many people use since it's more like a dumping ground, choked with garbage from the buildings nearby.

Dry garbage, the kind which doesn't begin to smell and, therefore, need not be cleared in a hurry: old newspapers, scraps of iron and broken furniture. So no one hears the body fall except for a cat which scurries away in fright.

After a while, even the cat returns, the blood congeals around the head, nothing moves as the night grows heavier and floods the lane with darkness washing away whatever chance there is for a stranger to discover the body.

A little later, a red handkerchief, folded neatly, falls from the terrace and halfway down a bit of it opens out, continues to fall, veering just a few inches from its path because of a light wind.

It comes to rest on the body, on his leg, inches above the knee and my sister walks down, free at last. There's a taxi waiting and she tells the driver to take her to what was once her home, in the neighbourhood where the pigeons lie sleeping in their cage.

GIRL TALK

'You should have seen their faces,' she says.

'What about their faces?' I ask.

She begins to laugh.

It's an April afternoon, so hot that it's not yet four, and from the balcony I have already seen two people whose slippers stuck to the tar on the street making them trip.

The nor'westers are late. The rain must have lost its way in the hills, deliberately, she says. The winds must have got bored stiff travelling the same route, the same sky, the same sea, year after year, and that's why this time they have decided to take a break.

We have closed the windows, she has wet two towels, draped one on each of the curtains. The ceiling fan is on, we have also set up a table fan which keeps moving from right to left, from left to right.

'Why do you need two fans?' I ask.

'Water evaporates, you idiot,' she says. 'It makes the room cool.'

She laughs, she laughs so hard that her eyes close, I can see her chest rise and fall, she throws back her head, I can see her neck, her hair, her teeth. The laugh crinkles her face, makes her cheeks almost touch her eyes. If I shut off the sound, it would seem she's crying, because I can even see the water collecting in her eyes.

I have never seen her laugh like this before, she now bends over, from the waist, holding on to the armrests of the cane chair, her hair falling over her face, I can see her eyes again, through the black strands, closed.

'You should have seen their faces,' she says.

'Stop laughing and tell me the story,' I say, mock angry, mock irritated.

And she purses her lips, makes a face, gets up from the chair and says she needs to take a break. She walks out of the room.

'Where are you going?' I ask.

She doesn't answer, just flings the drapes aside. I can hear her cough in the next room.

'Are you OK?' I ask, a bit worried at the sudden silence of her laughter.

And at that moment, she walks in. 'I have wiped the laugh off my face,' she says and she smiles. 'Now I can tell you the story.'

'How did you do that?' I ask.

'I remembered,' she says. 'But first, let me tell you what I told them.' And she begins.

* * *

There are four of us at the office. One, Two, Three, and myself, all pregnant, and every day, from Monday to Saturday, at one thirty in the afternoon, we sit down in the lunch room, at the same table, unpack our steel tiffin boxes, have lunch, and tell stories of our mothers-in-law. All of us, except me. I keep quiet. Because I have no problems with my mother-in-law. They want to know the secret but I evade the question.

One says her mother-in-law sleeps until 10 a.m. while she has to get up at five in the morning, do the dishes from the previous night, boil the water, make tea, knead the flour, make chapattis for her husband's tiffin, his father's breakfast, then serve bed tea, take her bath, wash her husband's dirty socks, iron his office clothes, super- vise the maid as she sweeps and scrubs the floors, ensure that the scrubwater has a few drops of Dettol, then dress up, run downstairs so that she can get the chartered bus to the office. And the moment One enters home at around 5.30 p.m., it starts again: cooking dinner, washing up, serving the food, wiping the dining table while the mother-in-law watches TV, father-in-law belches trying to read the day's newspaper, husband is asleep or with friends from office at some club, drunk, while she throws up at night, the baby moving inside. It better be a son, says One's mother-in-law.

Two says her mother-in-law isn't a slob, she cooks too, she washes the dishes and the clothes but only for her son, Two's husband. No more and no less. She will pack lunch for her son while Two has to cook hers, she will iron her son's clothes while Two will have to wait for the iron to be free and then hurriedly do hers. She will cook dinner in measured portions, precise, so that when her son has eaten, there's nothing left except the leftovers and Two will then have to boil an egg late at night when everyone is asleep, over the lowest flame so that the noise of the gas doesn't wake anyone up. Her baby needs its proteins and she buys an egg every day from the market near the office, hides it in her bag, along with the napkins, salt and pepper wrapped in paper which the mother-in-law never checks. All Two's mother-in-law wants is a boy.

*

Three says her husband beats her up and mother-in-law watches. Not real bad as in documentaries, just pulls at her hair or slaps her hard on the cheek. One day, her husband had come home from work and couldn't find the TV remote, told Three to look for it and while she was bending down on the floor, looking under the bed to see if the remote was there, he kicked her saying, 'Why don't you know where the remote is?' She fell, chipped her tooth, tasted her own blood and could hear mother-in-law sitting on the bed laughing, saying, 'Young women don't take care of their husbands any more.' He joins in saying he was a good football player when he was in school, doesn't mother remember that and mother says yes, that's why he can kick so hard. Sometimes, he beats her up just like that. Like when his friends had come and he told her to get the ice for the drinks and she said there had been a power cut and the icetray hadn't been refilled. And he got up from the living-room sofa, ran to her and hit her, she came crashing against the fridge and his friends were embarrassed and said they had to leave while mother-in-law looked straight into her eyes. 'Take care of his son inside you,' she said, 'get the ice from the market.'

*

143

Imagine my state. These are the three stories that get repeated every day with some frills added one day, something subtracted the next. Maybe they exaggerate but one thing is sure, these stories are the pillars on which they build, One, Two and Three, their dream house where for an hour every day, to the sound of lunch boxes being opened and closed, they live in peace, away from their mothers-in-law.

Surely, there are other things happening in our lives, like favourite TV shows, our bosses' philanderings, the other women in the office, the telephone receptionist who is having a love affair on the phone. And we do talk about these things, once I even told them about the old man and the pigeons, but the mothers-in-law sit, invisible, like three elephants in a tiny room and although you can turn your face away, forget that they are there, try to change the subject, whenever we look up, their huge shadows fall across the floor and you know that there's no escaping since the three elephants are all stacked up against the door.

At first, they asked me about my mother-in-law and I said things were OK, not so bad. 'What do you mean, Four? Tell us, Four, about her? Is she nice to you? What do you have to do to keep her happy? Doesn't she take sides when you fight with your husband? How is your husband, Four?'

The first few weeks, these questions kept buzzing round and round the table, like items from a women's magazine, and I kept flicking them away with smiles. And before these questions could start testing my patience, ironically, it was One, Two and Three who came to my rescue. They stopped asking me these questions.

Perhaps they realized I'm not the type who opens up, maybe they thought I'm going through worse, a hell so bad I can't even talk about it, and that I have a remarkable indifference to pain, I don't know. Or they thought, secretly, that I lived in that dream world where the daughter-in-law doesn't have to do a thing, she just adorns the house. Either way, they used me as a sounding-board, someone their age but at the same time some kind of elderly figure who's part counsellor, part friend, part sister, who has seen everything and, therefore, is above and beyond this daily cycle of anger and hate.

Until one afternoon, I decide that I have to do my bit too. When it's time, we all gather in the lunch room and I tell them to come close, and like little girls they follow my instructions and I tell them that what I'm about to say may shock them but they shouldn't shout or anything. They should only listen and they say, 'Yes, Four, we will do exactly as you say, we have been waiting for a long time to listen to your story and today is a very special day.'

I take a deep breath and I tell them that every night while they iron clothes, do dishes, chop vegetables, bend down to look for the remote under the bed, endure the insults and the jeers, I am away, far away in my bedroom, lying alongside my mother-in-law, our bodies wrapped around each other, she between my legs wiping away, with her lips and her tongue, whatever traces lie of the intruder: her son, my husband.

* * *

I tell her to lower her voice, what will the neighbours say.

But she laughs once again, it's all girl talk, she says, drawing me into it and we laugh and we laugh, the two of us together, until the sun begins to set, the towels on the windows dry, one falls off, the April afternoon slips into an April evening which then becomes an April night, the nor'westers knock at our window, waiting to be let in, but we have to keep them waiting since the lampshade may topple, break the stars moving on the blue bedspread which now flaps in the wind of two fans, one on the ceiling, one on the floor.

Straight Line

~⚭~

There's the white washbasin, there's the black iron hook and there's the brown hinge of the bedroom door. If you stand in the veranda, a couple of feet away from the wall, and look at these three things, you will discover that all three are in a straight line. Absolutely straight.

How important is this fact, I don't know.

Maybe it's just a coincidence, like the hundreds of other coincidences that need to happen to give this city its symmetry, its order. Or maybe it's nothing, just a storyteller's little twist to facts that are, to the rest of the world, of no consequence at all.

But I cannot let it pass.

Because it's the straight line, exact, mathematically precise, that strings the three scenes together. These are scenes from your mother's life and perhaps, in all the swirls and loops, the arcs and triangles of events and thoughts that make up my past, these three scenes are

147

held together by that straight line. Fixed, unable to bend or curl along with the others, unable to slip from memory to forgetting.

That's why when you begin to walk on your own, when you are tall enough to stand on the floor and reach the washbasin, I will bring you here. I will ask you to raise your arm, and keeping your fingers pressed to the wall, I will tell you to walk slowly, feel this straight line, the white chalk, the roughness of the wall, until you reach the end. So that in that one sweep of your little hand, your fingers would have touched the washbasin, the iron hook and the hinge on the bedroom door, the three points where three things happened to your mother and I.

First Point: *It's evening, still too early for the neighbour's TV set to laugh and sing. The sky is the six o'clock colour, between blue and purple. Sister is standing at the washbasin, the tap's running, I can hear the soap.*

It's late in the afternoon, Saturday, Sister is all dressed up to go somewhere. She has polished her slippers until their buckles shine. On the way back from school yesterday, she stopped at the shop, where we buy pencils and outline maps, to pick up a sachet of shampoo and lipstick.

Today, she's used both: her hair, black and smooth, falls over her shoulders. Her lips are red, she wears a blue skirt and a white top with tiny blue stars.

Sister never looked so beautiful.

She's told me her plan. She's told me her friends have bought tickets for the movie in Globe Cinema and after the movie they'll go to Flury's on Park Street to have an ice cream each. Her friend's brother has arrived from the United States, he'll also be there. He's smart, handsome, he's got a Casio synthesizer and he knows the tune to *Raindrops are falling on my window, teardrops are falling from my eye.*

I ask her if she is in love and she laughs, she kisses me, wipes the lipstick off my cheeks.

Father stumbles in at three, it's Saturday, half-day at work, he's louder than the traffic. I see him locking the door. Sister tells me to go to the other room and close my eyes, cup my hands to my ears. 'I will tell you when to see and when to hear,' she says. 'Until then, keep your eyes and your ears closed otherwise you will see the Wicked Witch in your dreams tonight.'

I do exactly as she tells me.

I hide in my favourite place behind the drapes and I

cheat. I listen through my fingers and I can hear Father asking her: 'Where are you going dressed up like a film actress?'

I cheat again, I keep one eye closed, open the other just a chink, and I see sister handing him the thin yellow slip of paper, jagged along one edge, it's see-through paper, I can see black lines and scribbles on it, it's her cinema ticket. Evening Show, five thirty to eight.

Father looks at the ticket and laughs, Sister smiles, he tears the ticket in two and laughs harder, he teeters for a while, tries to balance himself by holding my sister's shoulder and suddenly his face changes, he's not laughing any more, he's making a face as if he's in pain. And he throws up what I think he had for lunch. On sister's blue skirt, on her white top, in between the blue stars.

A drop spatters on the drapes where I stand. Both Father and Sister are laughing, Father begins to cough and then she leads him to the chair where he sits and she brings him a glass of water. And a huge red towel in which he wipes his face. He drinks the water, coughs to clear his throat, drops the two halves of the ticket onto the floor, where his lunch lies.

'Stay at home,' he says. 'It's too hot outside.'

It takes five minutes, this whole thing, and I am

scared Sister will find out that I saw and I heard. So I fling the drapes aside, run to the bedroom and lie down, close my eyes.

When I get up, it's an hour later, dark and quiet in the house. I need to wash the unslept sleep from my eyes, homework needs to be done, and I see Sister standing at the washbasin, we can hear the people, the cars and the buses from the streets. She has changed into house clothes, she is holding her blue skirt, one end in the white washbasin and she's scrubbing it with soap. She smiles and gestures to me to go away.

Second Point: *There's a bird cage hanging from the iron hook. Father and Sister both hold an old blanket and cover the cage. Then Father leaves and she stands there for a while, lifts one end of the blanket, blows a little kiss.*

'Why are you crying?' asks Father. And Sister tries to smile but she can't hide her tears, I am standing beside her, I can hear her heave deep breaths, her chest rising and falling.

'Why are you crying?' Father asks again, softly.

He's come back from work early and today his

breath is fresh, his glasses shine, his clothes smell nice. Outside, evening has fallen.

Sister sits down, at the dining table, I keep standing, Father's leaning against the door, still in his office clothes, and we listen to her tell us the story of the pigeon which flew out of the oil mill cage this morning and sat on the tram wire. She tells us about the No. 12 tram, from Esplanade to Galiff Street, which didn't stop. And when she comes to the bit about the old man shouting at the tram driver to stop and then shouting at the bird to fly away, fly away, she begins to cry again.

For some reason, although I don't care about the birds as much as she does, I too begin to cry and she puts her arm around me. Father leans over the table, pats us both. My sister on her shoulder, me on my head.

'Wait, you two,' he says and he leaves. We can hear him opening the door, we can hear the door close, he's going down the staircase, we can hear his steps, the scrape of his shoes.

Sister and I rush to the balcony, look down and we can see Father walking fast as if he has to catch a bus. He looks handsome, in his white shirt and dark trousers, walking with a purpose we have neither seen nor know about and Sister squeezes my hands and although we are crying, we are smiling as well.

Father turns into the lane which leads to the market and Sister takes me to the edge of the balcony, so close to the grille that I can smell the rust on the iron and she tells me to look but I can't see anything. She points at the manhole, turns me around, tells me to move a little to the left, a little to the right until I am exactly in line and there it is, the reddish-brown stain on the manhole cover, difficult to see in the dark but very clear in the headlights of approaching traffic.

'That's the pigeon,' she says, and we both look at the oil mill, the old man has gone, the cage is dark and quiet, the birds must have gone to sleep by now.

We wait for Father for half an hour or so and then sister tells me to go do my homework, sharpen my pencils for tomorrow, arrange the books and the exercise books in my bag, check my diary. There's nothing left to do, so I read the story book about the Far-away Tree again, evening slips into night, Bhabani is done with the dinner, we can hear her washing the dishes.

When I join Sister in the balcony again, she's still looking at the manhole, the reddish-brown stain is now a mere blotch. She's stopped crying, the tears have left lines on her face mixed with the dust from the iron grille but she still looks beautiful and we stand there, waiting for Father, watching the double-decker buses and the taxis pass by, their stream thinning down with the night.

I must have gone back, had dinner and gone to sleep because I don't remember what happened next until I woke up to a noise from the veranda.

Sister isn't in bed, I get up and walk to the veranda, her voice, soft and muted, mixed with a gentle fluttering as if wings had entered the house. And I am right, I see a brand-new cage hanging from a hook. And in the night, in the shadow of both Father and Sister, I see two white pigeons, baby pigeons, in the cage looking this way and that.

Sister covers the cage with an old blanket. She tells me that birds like to sleep in the dark and she blows a little kiss and we return to bed, we lie awake for a while, hear the flutter and the cooing of the two birds in the cage and Sister says they've come to our house for the first time and that's why they are so restless.

And we both close our eyes and thank Father from the bottom of whatever is left in our hearts.

Third point: *Father's gone, Bhabani is gone, I am so tall now that the washbasin comes to my waist, Sister's hair is still black and beautiful, the iron hook is still there but the cage is gone, the birds where I don't know.*

Your mother and I are leaning against the bedroom door, her left hand is on the hinge, her right is in mine, a nor'wester blows but the rain has stopped, the smell of wet earth and the wind run their fingers through her hair, there is a power cut outside, the sodium vapour lamps are switched off and we can, in the dark, see the stars. For some strange reason, even the garbage heaps have been cleared, the tram lines glint, it's like in happy stories and movies, the neighbourhood is as pretty as it should be when a brother and a sister meet, for one day and half a night, in fifteen years.

There's the white washbasin, there's the black iron hook and there's the brown hinge of the bedroom door. If you stand in the veranda, a couple of feet away from the wall, and look at these three things, you will discover that all three are in a straight line. Absolutely straight.

A CIRCLE

From a distance, it looks like a rubber band, the kind women use in their hair, but if you come close enough, you will see that it's a white circle, more like a ring, about an inch in diameter. Its rim is split, it's made of some kind of plastic, she can open it into a large semi-circle and when she lets go, it snaps back with a click you hardly hear.

'Where did you get this?' he asks.

'It's a curtain ring,' she says.

It fell in the maternity ward, onto the floor, when she tugged and tugged at the drapes, grey and heavy, to look out of the glass window. 'No one saw it fall,' she says, 'so I put it in my bag."

A brown leather bag with zips, long and short, opening and closing several pockets, big and small. The ring has been lying there, marking the years, holding her stories within its frame: the nurse at the hospital, her safety pin. Or the lights on Park Street, her husband standing on the terrace, his white shirt stretched tight across his back.

An hour ago she told him about the women at the office, their mothers-in-law, their tiffin boxes. Now she's playing with the ring, he looks at the fingers, longer than they once were, slender, there are now veins in her hands, like branches of a tiny tree pressed flat beneath her skin, the tufts of leaves the patches of wrinkled skin over her knuckles.

The ring falls to the floor, she doesn't notice, it rolls a little distance, bounces a fraction of an inch, trembles, comes to rest beneath the chair. He picks it up and while she continues with her story, he can see her hair, as it was, long, black and shining, and he says, 'Why don't you use the ring as a hairband?'

'Why don't you use the ring as a hairband?' he says again, holding it between his fingers, stretching and unstretching. She laughs and turns, he's looking at her back now and she says, 'Go ahead,' he gets up, leans forward, holds her hair, bunching it all in one hand, black and shining. She leans backward, he opens the white ring with his fingers and clasps it onto her hair, the ring stays, although it's split it doesn't give way, the circle is held intact by the weight of her hair, marking out the curve of her neck where once his head fitted exactly. More than twenty-five years ago.

VISITORS

DOMESTIC HELP

(Two stories in one)

In ten minutes, at the most fifteen, Bhabani will go. She
will leave our house after twenty years, her son has gone
to get the taxi, we are in the living room, she's sitting on
the floor, I'm on the chair, behind her I can see the past
in photographs, wooden frames on the wall. In the next
room is her little steel trunk, two bags and a water bottle.

Her son has got a job in Kharagpur, at the huge
railway yard, where they fix engines, check all electric
connections, the wheels, the tracks, before sending out
the trains on their journey to Calcutta and beyond.

She came to our house as a maid but there were a lot
more things than dishes to clean. She came as a young
woman, already grown up, but she grew up with us as
well, she was the one who shouted at Father when
someone needed to shout at him and although she didn't
live with us, she went every night, after dinner, to the

adjacent shanties where her husband and her children waited, she always left behind, in our house, something to mark her presence, to tell us that she would be back the next morning.

Sometimes, it was her slippers, sometimes, her earrings on the kitchen table, or a safety pin, a glass bangle. And on those nights when we couldn't play our blanket game or we couldn't set the stars free on the blue bedspread, we would look at these things and the night would pass.

Because she was a maid, she couldn't say much, she couldn't change much. So like the house, its walls and its floors, she stood and silently watched Father drink and laugh, Sister leave one night, Father die, I grow up. Any other maid would have left long ago, perhaps to go to some other household where the sound of dishes being washed mixed with the laughter of the family.

But Bhabani stayed.

And now she's leaving.

Ten minutes and she will be gone. There is not much to say, we are in the living room, she's sitting on the chair, I am on the floor.

'Tell me a story,' she says.

'I know how you came to this city,' I say. 'I know how you came into our house.'

She laughs. 'You will never know how I came here,' she says.

'I know,' I say.

'OK, tell me.'

'Listen,' I say, and she looks at me, with the same eyes with which she looked at me the first day she walked into this house.

'Wake up,' your husband says, 'wake up.' His hand is on your shoulder, he's shaking you hard. You open your eyes, the sari, bright yellow with red flowers, has slipped off your head, you draw it back, there's a Stranger standing three feet in front of you, near the door, brushing his teeth.

Your neck hurts, you sat all night on the floor of the 19 Up North Bihar Express, your back against the wooden frame of the passageway, your head bent to one side, your left ear pressed against your shoulder the whole night.

You stayed that way, for more than six hours, beginning midnight, when the train crossed Chittaranjan Junction. He told you that's where they make train engines, that's where Bihar ends, Bengal begins. 'Now you will see the names of the stations written in Bengali, Hindi is over,' he said.

You smiled admiringly, he knew so much.

'We are almost there,' he says.

You adjust your sari, jerk your head to the right, to the left, but the neck still hurts. You can taste the unfinished sleep in your mouth, you look at him drag the iron suitcase from below the berth. It's two weeks after your marriage, you are the only girl in the village who got your man from the city.

From where you sit you can see the door but only a part of it since it's blocked by the Stranger. He's wearing a sleeveless vest, a chequered towel around his waist, he keeps looking in the mirror above the steel sink as if he were looking at himself for the first time.

You check yourself, don't look at strange men in the city, your mother had said. So you lower the sari over your eyes, you can see the boy walk past with the tea, you can feel the warmth from his stove, the smell of milk, water and leaves.

You want a cup but you decide against it. You will need every rupee in the city.

*

The Stranger is taking his own time. You pull the sari further down, over your head, and then, cautiously, you look at him, the toothpaste foam dripping down his lips. Mother wrapped some food for you: pickles, vegetables and bread fried in ghee, enough to last you and your husband a couple of days.

You will not touch it right now because who knows how long it takes to get your own stove, who knows how far the kerosene shop, the market will be from the house. 'You never know distances in a city like Calcutta,' Mother had said.

He loves you, you are sure of that.

The first night you stayed up and he didn't touch you, just held your face in his hands and told you about his work in the city. His hands were soft, like a girl's.

'They are building a big house for very rich people and I am helping them build it,' he said. 'I work with men who come in yellow hats and they are very educated people. They have everything drawn on big sheets of paper.'

You didn't understand, how could they draw a picture of the house even before it was built? He laughed at the question, kissed you in reply, just like a hero in the movies. You blushed, gently pushed his face away.

He told you about Chowringhee, where little boys sell stuff made in foreign countries, watches and small machines which you could put in your pocket, on which you could do arithmetic, add and subtract big numbers. He told you about the shops where they have mannequins exactly like foreign women, with hair, eyes, noses, everything.

One day, he told you, there will be trains which will run in tunnels below the ground, whose doors will open when you have to get out and close as soon as you get in. By themselves, automatic. Above the train, will be the city, the road. And on top, buses, motorcars and people.

He told you about the Grand Hotel, the guards at the door, dressed up like kings in history books, silk turbans and moustaches, guards who earn more than anyone in the village.

'On Sunday, I have no work,' he said. 'We'll go to see these places.'

The Stranger is still brushing his teeth but now he has moved away from the door, he's moving closer to the lavatory and you lower your head, peer out.

The train seems to have slowed down, you can hear the whine of the wheels, through the door you can see walls, red houses, the railway quarters, huge piles of garbage pass by. Behind you, a hawker walks down the aisle, balancing himself as the train moves, selling ball-point pens, red, black and blue.

'Look, look,' your husband says.

And he points outside, you hold one edge of one seat, get up, move closer towards the door, you look outside and through the morning mist, over the red officers' quarters, you can see the iron girders of the Howrah Bridge, the one everyone in the village seemed to know about, the bridge waiting, like a friend, to take you across, into the city.

Both of you are standing at the entrance of the coach, man and wife, looking at the bridge. You can feel his hand against yours, the smell of his sweat mixing with that of the tea and the Stranger's toothpaste and the train, you can hear the water in the sink.

You will see all the places your husband told you about, you will go to Chowringhee, look at the mannequins, the guards at the hotel.

But before all that, just two days after you step into the city for the first time, you will walk, nervously, into a three-bedroom house, across from an oil mill.

You will meet two children, a girl and a boy, and their father. And you will spend the rest of your time there, standing guard at our door, at our windows, to keep love from running away. Your husband will keep flitting from one construction site to the other, watching the buildings go up in the city.

'That's it, Bhabani,' I say. 'Isn't this how you came to this city, to this house?'

'Who was that Stranger in the train?' she asks.

'This is a story, Bhabani, the Stranger was a stranger,' I say.

'Who could he be?'

'Someone who lived in this city and was returning that morning in the same train.'

'Where will he be now?'

She smiles, she's pulling my leg, she gives me her hand, asks me to help her get up.

'It's a nice story,' she says. 'I will remember it.'

'What do you mean?' I ask.

'It's a nice story,' she says again. 'And it's also not entirely wrong because in reality it was also something like that, we came to Calcutta in the train, we saw the bridge in the morning.'

She stops, turns.

'What is it, Bhabani?' I ask.

'Nothing, I remembered something and then I forgot,'

she says, turns back and goes to the next room to pick up her bags.

Her son is waiting downstairs in the taxi to take his mother away and she walks out of the room, everything is packed, her brown steel trunk, two bags and a water bottle.

And as she gets into the taxi, unsure, her son holding her hand, she turns to me and says, 'You know why I am leaving, I know you can take care of yourself now, I can go.'

The taxi revs up its engine, the doors slam shut, she's turned her face away from me, her son waves his hand, all I can hear is the sound of her mallet, which I once used as a cricket bat, beating the dirt out of our clothes. And all I can see in front of my eyes, through my tears, is Bhabani walking up the stairs, two children following her, in their school uniform, to the terrace, all three holding a wet blue bedspread, like the velvet curtain of a cinema hall, and then spreading it out to dry.

CABLE TELEVISION

The camera glides from one body to the other, all wrapped in green see-through plastic, there's an ambulance, its doors open, the huge red cross discoloured, split, making each half of the door look like a piece in some sad jigsaw puzzle.

The Serbs shelled a market place in Sarajevo forty-five minutes ago killing more than sixty, mainly women and children. There's a crowd watching the aid workers and he can see her in the last row, behind the reporters, behind the three UN men. She stands looking away, at something that's off the screen. He sees a flash of red, it's her scarf, her eyes are as blue as the TV screen at the end of the day's programming, just before the coloured bars pop up.

He is the man in the upstairs flat who beats up his wife but tonight he has to see the Sarajevo Woman again so he sits through the entire news bulletin, the full twenty minutes, right through the hour's top stories: hyperinflation in Argentina, Clinton in trouble, nothing in Calcutta, the inspectors in Baghdad, the Vietnamese teenagers in jeans, on motorcycles, and when they return to Bosnia they show the bodies again, talk to a UN official in Geneva over the phone, they show the ambulance but not his Sarajevo Woman.

He flicks the TV off, he likes watching the image collapse into a bright speck that glows fiercely for a fraction of a second before it dissolves into the greyness of the screen. It reminds him of a shooting star. The next bulletin is one hour away.

Ever since he got a cable connection for two hundred rupees a month he cannot sleep until it's past two, sometimes even past three in the morning. For a thousand rupees, a fifth of his salary, the cableman gave him a remote and he keeps flicking the channels with the volume on zero because he doesn't want to wake up his wife, fast asleep in the next room, who wakes up at the slightest of sounds, even that of a remote control accidentally falling to the floor.

*

He steps into the veranda that overlooks the main road.

To his left is the terrace, common to all the families in the building, but hardly ever used. Sometimes, from the downstairs flat, a man comes to the terrace holding a blue bedspread, spreads it out to dry, two clips on either side, one white and the other red.

Tonight, however, there's nothing on the terrace, the lights in the man's room are burning.

From down below, from the pavement, he can hear the men turn in for the night; the wooden cots being dragged, someone gargling, spitting; the clang of iron buckets being plopped down on the pavement. The buses have to be washed.

The landlord owns four 30B buses, the longest and most lucrative route in the city, all the way from Dum Dum Airport to Outram Ghat: right through the busiest market in Sealdah, the office district in Dalhousie Square, past the jetty where steamers leave for Howrah railway station every fifteen minutes.

The buses have returned, stained and streaked, the conductors half asleep, their leather bags slung over their shoulders, hunters coming home with their dead birds.

He likes to watch the buses being washed, to hear the drops of water sizzle against the engines. Buckets and buckets until the conductors get tired, give up, sleep on the Ladies' Seat as the buses drip until dawn.

The next morning, *The Statesman* has the picture on page one. 'Death comes shopping in Sarajevo market', the headline. The photo caption: *A Sarajevo father mourns the loss of his son in a Serb mortar attack in a market place yesterday afternoon. At least 60 people were killed.*

The father in the photograph wears a thick black tweed coat with grey stripes; his eyes are closed, his head is thrown back, his mouth half open. Two of his upper teeth are missing, he's crying. To his left is an elderly woman, perhaps his mother, the dead child's grandmother. She's crying, too, holding his left arm firmly, so firmly that the coat's sleeve is pushed almost off his shoulder. And behind her, is his Sarajevo Woman.

The picture is black and white so he can't make out the colours but there's no mistaking those eyes, big and deep; that scarf around her beautiful neck. He can see more of her now: the bridge of her nose, her straight, black hair falling just below her shoulders.

He steps out of the office at five, the newspaper in one hand, his Sarajevo Woman resting against his knee, moving up and down with each step, his imitation leather suitcase in the other.

On any other day, he would have waited at the bus stop, watched the municipal trucks scoop the garbage off the corner, dump it into their vans, like elephants eating at the zoo.

Or he would have watched the crowd at the bus stop, each person doing something, the woman adjusting her sari, the girl walking up and down, the men looking at their watches. He would have noticed the tarpaulin roofs of the slums flutter in the wind; the film posters stuck to the walls, one on top of another, all torn in different places.

But today all that fades in the shimmering haze of the afternoon as he keeps walking, his head down, his eyes locked on to the shifting patch of the street below, the gobs of spit, twisted cigarette ends, a baby sleeping, stones, and finally his door.

He waits for his wife to go to sleep and when he can hear her breathe, see her chest rise and fall in the dark, he undresses, lifts the TV on to the bed, its screen staring at the ceiling, the white cable wire stretched taut against his black pillow.

Today, the Serbs have held about fifty UNPROFOR

men captive. And behind the white hospital building, where ambulances are parked in a line, like schoolboys in a drill, she sits, wearing a blue skirt that reaches her ankles, a white shirt and the same red scarf.

Her blue eyes stare straight into his face as he hugs her, his lips move over her, he can see the veins in her hands, her nails painted pink, the fuzz on her lips, he kisses her hard, the camera moves and her head rests against his chin, he can smell the dying city in her hair.

He wants to ask her several questions, why was she sitting at the hospital, what was she doing in the market place, does she know that father mourning the loss of his son in the picture. He wants to help her get out, but it's too late, Bosnia is gone, will be back in another half an hour.

Outside, they have started washing the buses; inside, his wife turns in her sleep, the marks of his fingers on her cheeks, and he looks at the double lines his lips have left in the dust on the TV screen.

AMERICAN DREAM

In the centre of the city, where buses and trams begin and end their routes, not far from where Sarah Parker once lived, there's a huge building the colour of chocolate, its windows black glass, its steps black marble, smooth and shining, like your mother's hair.

When the city becomes a desert, hot and lonely, when wherever you look, it all looks the same and the wind blows sand into your eyes, this building is an oasis.

When the city becomes an ocean, wet and heavy, when the crowds are waves hammering your body, pulling you down, this building is an island.

For here they come, walking or swimming, at first, in ones and twos. And then in twos and threes, every five minutes or so, until half an hour later there's a small crowd.

Men and women, eighteen to fifty years old, some even sixty or seventy, holding on to the railing for support, brushing the sand off their clothes, wiping the spray from their face.

It must have been bad last night, maybe they couldn't sleep, the fans were still, the lights off. There was a power cut in the neighbourhood, they spent the night fanning themselves with the newspaper, rolled up, looking at the clouds, through the iron grille in their windows, hurriedly travel across the moon.

Or perhaps they had nothing to do, they just sat in the balcony and watched the pigeons flutter in the cage across the street, tried to identify what was there in the garbage heap: cracked plastic buckets, vegetable peels, clumps of women's hair dropped off combs.

They all walk up the steps, careful in case they slip; their shoes, slippers slide on the smooth marble, washed and scrubbed at least four times a day. They shuffle in, past the metal detector, a couple of beeps for the cigarette boxes, the keys, they walk past the uniformed guards, to wait in the lobby.

They look at the latest posters from the Museum of Modern Art, a splash of colour behind the glass frame. Or the photograph poster from NASA, blue-black, dark and cool, with some planet and some stars.

While they wait, they tilt their heads to look at the

ceiling, they can see the city's sky through the glass, white at this time of the day. They are called in, one by one, they open their bags, they can see the sand covering the brass buckle, their handkerchiefs drenched in the ocean's waves. They bring out their IDs, college fee books, company cards. A woman in a skirt with a laminated card around her neck, like a necklace, takes down their names. She then goes to the computer, they hear her type, some bend to see their names come up on the screen, letter by letter, the cursor flashing at the end.

She peels off the barcode stickers from a roll, pastes them onto the cards, they sign, their elbows leave sweat marks on the glass-top counter. Carefully, so that no one can see, they wipe it with their shirt sleeves. The cards are ready.

They scatter all around. Some sit on the beige sofa, let the body sink into the leather, some lean against the steel backrest, cold against the skin. Their shoes are covered with sand or spray, they pull their feet in underneath the tables, embarrassed, so that no one can see.

The sweat begins to evaporate; outside, the wind continues to blow across the desert, the waves continue to churn in the ocean, through the Venetian blinds in the window, they can see the air shimmer as if in a mirage, the little boy selling lemonade, the sun winking off the glasses.

The Stars and Stripes droops in the heat like a huge handkerchief put out to dry.

They get last week's *New York Times Sunday Magazine*, look at the Georges Marciano girls in black skirts and tight white shirts waiting to be kissed. They peel off the perfume strips on the next page, rub their wrists and smell themselves.

They go to the bathroom, stepping lightly on the green carpet, the cold faucet is blue, the warm is red, they wash their faces, pour out the liquid soap that floats, like cool green jelly, in their palms. They tear out the tissue paper for the first time in their lives, watch it stain dark in patches as it soaks in the water from their washed hands.

On the way back to the sofa, they stop near the Fiction section to drink water. Chilled water in pretty little styrofoam cups. They return, cool and fresh, their wrists smelling of Elizabeth Taylor's perfume, they can see the black man in the Ralph Lauren shirt, they touch his chiselled face.

Now it's time to choose their apartment in Central Park West with a spiral staircase, French doors, sun-filled elegance, a gorgeous granite kitchen with maple mantles. And as they keep flipping the pages, the perfume rises; they can hear the air conditioner hum, the cool draft blowing across their face and their eyes; through the drapes they can see flashes of the sun outside.

The lemonade boy has gone, leaving behind a patch of water fast disappearing on the pavement, the apartment in Central Park is now a sprawling house in Long Island, the snow covers the field and with the magazine still open, the Mazda, with the airbags, to the left, the Banana Republic woman to the right, they fall asleep.

Half an hour and they will get up, put the magazines back in the places they came from. And they will walk out of the American Center Library into a city which is no longer a desert or an ocean, they will get into buses, no sign of the sand or the spray, each will go his or her way. Back to their homes to wait for the power cut, to watch the clouds hurriedly travel across the moon. Or listen to the pigeons fluttering in the cage and look at the empty street, black and shining, like your mother's hair.

Baby Food

There's not much in the fridge, let me remember. Just a couple of potatoes, old, with things, some curly, some straight, coming out of their skins. A bottle of ketchup, its cap stuck because of the crust. There's a lettuce, cut and chopped, its leaves dry, what remains of its head quivers every time the fridge coughs.

There's not much in the kitchen cabinets either. Or in the spice jars, just two sticks of cinnamon, smelling like my breath when I have fever. There's one egg, an onion, I could scramble it, fry it, but I'm too tired to cook now, there's a pouch of toned milk I got two days ago. That should do.

I will have to get up in five minutes, take a break, let the pen rest for a while, the ink on its nib breathe in the night air, let the words sleep before they are called once again to perform to our bidding. For there's a long way to go.

First, I have to wash the smell of the hospital from my face, my hands. In my hurry to get down to these stories, I forgot to remove my socks; the nylon and the sweat, the water heater doesn't work, the water must be cold.

How long will you remain in that towel? No, I'm not going to disturb you now, when you wake up in the morning, we'll change you, clean you up, get breakfast ready.

Once upon a time we had the Calcutta Milk Corporation Van, white and blue, dented, strips of steel bent and jutting out, but it came tearing down the street as if it was brand new. It lurched, shuddered over potholes, the milk inside was kept in aluminium cans so the driver didn't care, let them rattle against each other. So that half an hour before sunrise, the Van woke up the neighbourhood, first the pigeons in the cage, then the birds in the trees and then all of us.

The Van stopped a few years ago, now they've set up a milk booth down the street where people begin lining up one full hour after sunrise, their eyes wide open as they drop coins and wait for the light to turn green, for the milk to flow, precisely measured, gurgle into their steel cans, drip drip at the end, the froth collecting at the top of the jar, spilling over when they put on the cover. I skip all this, I buy the pouch.

I shall boil this milk; I've seen mothers on TV test the milk against their wrists, I shall do the same and when it's cool, when I am sure it won't hurt your lips, I shall feed you the milk, I shall pour the milk into your mouth carefully so that the rim of the spoon, its steel edge, doesn't scrape your gums. And I shall hold the spoon close to my chest so that if you wish to, you can imagine I'm your mother and the milk flows, drop by drop, from her breast.

Maybe my hands will shake, I am not a young man any more, your head may jerk and the spoon may tilt, the milk will run down my shirt but it doesn't matter, it's milk, cool to the touch, I can always wash up later. What's important is you don't miss your mother tonight.

BROTHER

ALL ALONE

At first, we try the cinema hall.

Three days of the week, Monday, Wednesday and Friday, I leave the office exactly at five, wait for her at the crossing of Amherst Street and Bowbazar, right in front of the Lady Dufferin College and Hospital. Around five thirty, after her anatomy class, she walks out. My Princess, tall and dark, with a black leather bag, its strap running over her left shoulder, between her breasts, up her back.

Her hair catches the wind, bounces off her shoulders like that of the shampoo girls on TV when they twirl on their toes.

Above the swirling crowd of patients, pregnant women and sick children hanging on to their fathers' index fingers, between the ambulances with streaks of metal showing through the paint, against the yellow building with dirty glass windows, her face floats like that of an angel in the sky.

My heart aches.

*

I have already paid the rickshaw, told him where to go, how to go. Without a word, we hop on, take the short cut via Sonagachi, the city's largest whorehouse, watch the pimps scratch themselves, the prostitutes' children play with the cows, poke them in the udders with broomsticks, the NGO girls counting condoms, we reach Grace Cinema, College Street, buy two dress circle tickets, pay fifteen rupees extra for the back row, wait for the lights to go down, for the commercials to get over, the house to settle down.

Until it's dark, as dark as a moonless night, except for two faint stars, the EXIT signs, one on either side, glowing like two red boils on black skin; the usher's torch bobs up and down like a glow-worm lost its way.

She wears a skirt.

She always wears a skirt on our cinema nights. To let me slip my left hand between her legs. No unbuttoning of buttons, no noise of zips being unzipped. Nobody hears her skirt ride over her knees; she's dark, I'm dark, the cinema hall is dark and so nobody notices my left hand press her right knee.

As the credits begin to roll, my fingers move up her leg. Her skin, smooth up to where she rubbed the cream after her bath. By the time the music director's name appears on the screen, I can feel her legs clench, her legs give way.

I slide my fingers deep, through the warmth, through the wetness. And when they slip in, I write I L-O-V-E Y-O-U on the inner wall inside her, letter by letter. By the time I reach the second O, she's trembling.

She writes too: I L-O-V-E Y-O-U T-O-O on the terry-cotton fabric of my trousers, Rs 125 per metre, stretched tightly over my hardness. Our passions peak, the movie begins, we get up and walk out.

She has to be home by seven, her mother is waiting. My trousers are stained so I pull my shirt out, let it fall below the waist. It doesn't look good, the end of the shirt, all crumpled up, but it covers the evidence.

On our way out, we stand in the lobby of the theatre to look at the stills of the movie before we step out into the city's falling light. I see her off at the bus stop and walk home.

On the fourth evening, the usher sees us; that too by accident. His torch slips out of his hand, he bends over to pick it up and as he raises himself, the glowing torch in his hand, the light falls on us. On my left wrist, on her right thigh.

Our cinema nights are over.

*

So we try the park. It's not exactly a park, just a clearing in the block of moss-covered buildings near St Paul's School, less than a mile from her medical college, heading north. We reach there, there's a football game on, schoolboys, in blue shorts and white shirts, some with ties, some barefoot, their shoes, piled up, used to mark the goalposts.

We stand near the rusted iron turnpike at the entrance, our lust buzzing so hard we are afraid someone may hear. A mother sits on the iron bench, in front of us, so that we can reach out and touch her, admiring her son play, tying and untying the plastic strap of his water bottle around her fat fingers.

The sun has fallen behind the school's church, the street lights have been switched on but they burn uselessly against the bright sky, the sun falling but still pretty strong, stretching the boys' shadows to absurd lengths. We stand there, now leaning against the turnpike, now straight. She takes out her tiffin box and we share her lunch.

Two slices of bread separated by a thick omelette drenched in tomato ketchup and lots of fried onions spread in between.

While we eat, we watch the shadows rather than the boys. Tall, thin, dark forms flitting across the park in the falling light of day, mixing and merging, touching our legs, floating over the iron railings onto the road, sometimes even underneath the bus.

By six, the boys have gone, the park is empty, the mother with the water bottle has gone.

We sit down on the bench, today she wants me to write on her breasts. My left hand moves up, beneath her red top with black stripes. The fingers slow down over her vertebrae, speedbreakers on the road of her back, before unclasping her bra, unclasping its hooks.

And then the hand moves, across her back, below the armpit, feels the gentle brush of its hair until it reaches her breast, my writing pad. She is leaning against me now, my fingers trace the curve, write, move between her breasts to the base of her neck, up her voice box to where her chin starts and she leans her head backwards, I smell her hair, black and shining, and I am about to close my eyes when I see a child walk into the park, a ragpicker.

He picks up scraps of paper that maybe fell from the schoolboys' pockets. Maybe someone dropped, during the game, a sheet of paper with all the answers. Or all the questions for homework. There will be one worried-to-death child in the city tonight.

The child looks at me and smiles, keeps picking up whatever he can find and when his hands are full, he drops the bunch into a huge gunny bag that he drags across the ground. Behind him, the lights are coming on in the balconies of the flats as wives emerge to collect the washed, dried clothes before their husbands come home.

On our third evening, a police constable walks into the park to pee. She sees him first, jerks back, pushes my hand out of her top, puts her bag on my lap to cover my hardness, it is too late.

We try everything.

The service lane behind the college but the children use it for their cricket matches; the Sealdah vegetable market, right at the end of the row of vegetable shops where they sell coloured fish and baby parrots which can talk. The problem is there are too many cockroaches there.

One day, she even sneaks us into her anatomy lab, we go down on the floor between the tables on which two cadavers lie, one on each table, one grinning, one with no face at all. A headless body. But the smell of formaldehyde makes me throw up and we spend all our time trying to wipe the muck away.

Until she comes up with the Idea.

And one evening, we don't meet outside her college but go straight to her house. I hold her mother while she injects her with something I don't know. Mother kicks, mother screams, I push my hand in her mouth, she bites hard, I stifle my scream, it doesn't matter, it has to be done, the traffic drowns the noise as my Princess takes the scalpel from her leather bag and I turn my face away while she does what has to be done. It's all over in just under thirty minutes, even the dressing, the cotton gauze drenched in disinfectant, wrapped like a blindfold, mother fast asleep.

I ask her no questions as we tear at each other's clothes, our love mixes with our crime, dissolves, like an ice cube out of the freezer, in the smell of her bedsheet, the musical clock on her wall, the mercurochrome stains on her fingers, the noise of the trams, and most important of all, my Princess next to me, undisturbed.

As for those eyes that float in the Horlicks jar, she will know what to do.

DIAL TONE

One night, in the same room in which you sleep, where the pillows are, I sat there, looking at the phone, the same black phone which rang tonight, the same black cord, the only difference, its spirals were closer together, tighter, the black was blacker, the steel rings on the dial shone white, like silver newly polished.

Every ten minutes or so, I kept checking to see if the phone was working.

Our neighbourhood wasn't part of an electronic exchange, there were no twenty-four-hour telephone booths, with glass cubicles, at street corners. And quite often the phone would die, suddenly, so that when you picked it up, you couldn't hear the dial tone of its breath, just a strange silence sometimes broken by a buzz or a rustle.

She was going to call me that night, my Princess, tall and dark, the phone was alive.

Once I was in love in the only way I could be in this city.

I was younger then, this house had already emptied its two hearts into the city, Father and Sister, one was dead, the other had gone. Bhabani was still there, she had washed and ironed the blue bedspread, kept it away in the cupboard, rolled tiny mothballs into its folds. For some reason, I had begun to like only black and white.

The bedspread gone, I had got myself a new bedsheet. Black with a giant white conch shell drawn in the centre and tiny white conch shells all around the four sides of its rectangle.

The TV was black and white, they kept showing an Australian movie, late in the night, where the actress, white, wore a velvet gown, black, and she looked through the window at a garden covered with snow, there was a black coffin in the middle of the garden, all around its four edges, were black stones.

The phone rings, I am lying on the bed, on my stomach, my hands pressed like sepals against my face, I push the newspaper away, black and white, I lean forward and pick up the phone, my chest presses against the conch shell, the black stones in the garden, I begin talking.

I tell her that I am happy, safe, that I am ready to take on this city with her by my side. I will soon get a job that will pay me well, my house is exactly the kind she tells me stories about, it has warm towels and cool sheets, the bathroom is dry, the soap smells nice, the taps don't drip.

I tell her she can do up the house any which way she wants, change the rooms, make the living room the bedroom, the bedroom the study, it doesn't matter, all that matters is that she come and live with me, her mother won't watch us any more, we can go to cinema halls to watch the movie, not look for the usher's torch. We will go to the park to watch schoolboys play football, the goalposts marked with their shoes. And stand there, hand in hand.

We shall keep our love for the house, not for the city, I say. We can go to the Howrah station to watch the local trains leave in the morning, sleep in front of the Victoria Memorial until it's time to go home.

And while I am telling her all this, my words soft and loving, flowing as if in a torrent let loose, the fan cuts the air in thick slabs that drip onto my body, onto the bed-sheet, a fly comes from nowhere, to rest on the receiver, black on black, I brush it away, it returns, 'What's happened?' she asks.

'Nothing,' I say, and I continue talking and I tell her that she is the woman I love, and like the long-awaited rain, she has filled the cracks of my life, washed the dirt away.

'So will you marry me?' I ask.

'Let's see,' she says.

We never met again. She stopped calling, and for the next few months I kept running to the phone whenever I thought I heard it ring but then it was only the tram. Or the bus conductor jangling the bell. Sometimes it was nothing, just in my head.

Like lonely lovers often do, I kept thinking things, I conjured up worlds where we were husband and wife, we had taken a house, all for ourselves, with a tiny garden in front.

And for quite a while, every day, I kept drawing and redrawing the same scene, filling it out with colours and noises.

It's evening and I am sitting on my chair, my legs raised on a table, I am reading aloud to her. Outside, our child lies on his stomach, in the garden, he's playing with a twig, a leaf, an ant.

And while he is playing, he keeps staring at us, through the window where there are tall white curtains billowing in the wind.

She laughs at something I have read and I tell her, 'Let me finish and then you laugh as much as you want to.' She laughs again, I get irritated but I know it's time to call in the child since it's getting late and we all are eating out tonight.

So I close the book, get up, walk to my wife, and we both go to the window and call out to our child, we can see him drop the twig, look at us, smile, and we can hear his feet on the steps, he walks into our arms.

It's a scene I have squeezed into fiction now, best played out only in our minds. For if she had said yes that night, if we lived in a house with a garden in front, I might never have been in this neighbourhood, I wouldn't have been here when your mother came on that April night, you wouldn't have come to this city.

STRONG WIND

No one noticed.

It was seven in the evening and the wind was so light that no one saw the curtains rise and fall a fraction of an inch. No one heard, above the noise of the double-decker buses and the trams, the taxis and the trucks, the leaves tremble in the topmost branches of the banyan tree across the street.

No one stood in the balcony and looked below, through the iron grille, to wonder why the garbage heap was quivering as if some strange animal, small and wild, were trapped inside.

Why bits and pieces of trash, the lighter ones, had begun to break free and move in small circles at first and then slowly in large spirals until one, a slip of paper, reached the tram tracks in the middle.

Surely, someone out there, on the street, across the Hooghly, on the Howrah Bridge, someone in this city of twelve million people, must have noticed it.

Or even felt it.

Certainly, some tired passenger, on his way home from work, standing on the footboard of the tram, his copy of the newspaper or his imitation leather suitcase flapping like a bird against his knee, must have felt a sudden draught against his face.

Or a little child staring out of a bus window must have pushed his hand out, just like that, and felt the wind run through his fingers. And when his father told him, 'Don't do that, it's dangerous, pull your hand inside,' the child must have turned his face away, embarrassed at the reprimand in public, and then just as he turned his face he would have felt the wind in his hair.

But then in this city, even a child, at times, doesn't notice the wind.

She will run away tomorrow.

She has prepared for it. For the last three years, she has been walking to college, saving the money her father gives her for the bus fare and for tiffin. She prefers notes, not coins, it's easier to keep the notes in the Bata shoe carton she uses as her make-up box. With the lipstick, the three shades of nail polish, and four pairs of earrings.

Using differently coloured rubber bands, she separates the one-rupee notes from the twos, the fives and the tens.

She doesn't count every day, like Silas Marner she's read about, she just keeps putting the notes in their respective bundles. She knows what she will wear tomorrow: the blue skirt with a white top with tiny blue stars. She wants to look good but she doesn't want to get noticed. He will wait at the College Street intersection.

She has got it all worked out, she will get up in the morning, wait for the newspaper man to throw the paper into the house, wait for her father to read the editorials, finish his tea, go for shopping. The thick wooden door makes a lot of noise so when Father leaves she will not shut the door behind him.

She will wait until she hears the sound of his footsteps change, from the sharp clap clap of rubber on stairs to the gentle shuffle shuffle when he reaches the landing. Then, two or three minutes later, she will pull the door gently, keeping it slightly ajar so that when the time comes, no one will hear, no one will notice.

But first she will wait for the maid to go into the kitchen, begin breakfast, she will wait until she hears the kettle being put on the gas stove, the click of the lighter, the pop of the flame. And when she is staring at the oil in the pan, watching the sides curl up, the first bubbles rise to the surface, she will run away.

With the notes stuffed at the bottom of her bag, all of the three thousand rupees, covered with some of her clothes, the nicer ones, she will walk into the waiting taxi and leave what has been her world for the last nineteen years. Never to return.

The wind picks up. It lifts the blue plastic mug from the garbage heap, tosses it two to three feet, lets it roll into the drain where it comes to rest against a brick. It whistles through the banyan tree, slips in through the cracks in the window, lifts the curtains, topples the wooden doll on the television set, the two tiny glass ducks in the showcase, cracking one beak.

Bhabani is standing in the kitchen watching the oil snap, the wind teases her hair, blows the onion peels across the floor, dries the sweat on her back. Father is sitting in the living room, back from work, leaning over to untie his shoelaces. He rolls his grey socks to his ankles before pulling them off, the wind blows in through his toes.

I sit on the bed, my khaki schoolbag half open, the wind catching the corners of the *Oxford University Atlas*. In front lies my geography homework, the outline map of Italy waiting to be filled up. Genoa and Rome as little black dots; the Adriatic Sea in blue, I begin colouring the sea but the wind grows stronger, the waves rise, the map turns over, flaps against my felt pens, I use the geometry box as a paperweight.

I can hear Father in the bathroom, the flush, the water being sucked into the drain, the splash as the mug falls into the bucket. Moments later, the flick of the bathroom switch being switched off, Father's wet Hawaii chappals slapping against the cement floor as he walks into the dining room to listen to the nine o'clock news on his Philips radio.

I hear the wind rattle the windows, bang them shut.

But no one notices. She skips dinner saying her stomach hurts. She goes to her room, lies down in her bed and closes her eyes. She has to get a good night's sleep since it will be a long day tomorrow. She's not scared, not nervous although she's never lived on her own before, never lived outside her house.

Over the last few days she's felt an energy in her body, in her hands, her eyes, her legs, the source of which she doesn't know. So while she does, on the surface, all that's expected of her to do, she is also building her future far away from this house, with the man she thinks she loves.

She slips into half-sleep, hears the first drops of rain fall into the blue plastic mug that lies in the drain.

It rained for three nights and four days. The wind snapped the tram wires, they hung dangerously low, just a few feet from the water which by now covered the fuse boxes of the lamp-posts. The flood, the first in more than twenty-five years, swallowed everything that came in its way: the garbage heap, the shanties on Amherst Street and Kalighat, two girls on College Street, an entire bus near Outram Ghat, all the benches in the park near St Paul's School.

On the second day, they brought the boats out, swaying under the weight of kind men and women. The taxi didn't come, couldn't come, she didn't run away.

She ran away only three days later when the water was gone leaving behind a layer of silt that draped the city like a fine blanket, creased and folded where people walked, stomped their feet. The sun came out, the Corporation worked overtime to clean the manholes, all clothes in the city were dank, a musty smell hung in the neighbourhood and she walked away, this time into the night, when everyone was asleep, with a man I hope she loved.

As for me, I just walked around the house between long periods of sleep. School was called off and I re-did the map of Italy, this time more carefully. There was not much to do in the kitchen since the stock of vegetables ran out, we ate biscuits, puffed rice and kept listening to the radio. The announcers couldn't come to the office so they kept playing the same music again and again. We slept for long hours in the afternoon, listening to the water outside and in the evening, came out in the balcony and watched the dying sun bounce off the sheet of water that stretched as far as we could see.

We have let the present fill us up, we have pushed the past to whichever corner it can. We have told each other about those three nights and four days when the floods came to the city. About how she couldn't run away and how I ate biscuits, did my geography homework and listened to the news on the radio. And although there's nothing common in our experiences since then, nothing that we can call shared, both of us know that both of us noticed the wind and we knew, long before the world did, that it was a strong wind.

Perhaps, it was this that finally brought us together, even if it was for a day and half a night.

THE HIGHWAYMAN

'I'm scared,' she says.

'Of what?' he asks.

'Of the baby in the bathroom.'

'What baby?'

She has told him this story many times but he says he always forgets. So she begins again.

His ink was red, a smooth, glistening red; his paper was white. And when he finished writing a page, it looked like a picture postcard. Of a miniature garden, in a foreign country, covered with snow and red flowers.

Every day, except Sunday, I would go to him, with my exercise book and a red pen, so that he could write and I could take some of these picture postcards home. He was my English Literature tutor, I was in school when there wasn't much literature to teach or learn.

So we kept reading our favourite lesson, the poem

called 'The Highwayman', and although it was an easy poem, I knew it by heart, I knew what it meant, I always asked him to read it out to me.

The moon was a ghostly galleon tossed upon cloudy seas, the road was a ribbon of moonlight upon the purple moor. And the highwayman came riding, riding, riding, the highwayman came riding up to the old inn door.

I called him Sir, he didn't charge us anything. Sir worked as an accountant at a bank in the city; why he taught me, I don't know. Once he said he liked reading poems and stories. He lived in a two-room house, about ten minutes on foot from our neighbourhood, with his wife and a three-year-old baby girl.

Every day, after we were done with our lessons, the homework questions taken care of, he and his wife would go shopping and ask me to take care of the girl until they returned. So for the next half-hour or so I would become part sister, part mother. I would make up stories, tell her about kings and queens, about the prince who went out one day into the forest, about the trees that go wisha wisha wisha at night.

Once I began telling her about the highwayman, the moon in the sky, the old inn door, but the night frightened her, she began to cry. So I made the highwayman funny, I made him into a clown jumping up and down a yellow-coloured road.

Sometimes we played a game with her shirt. She always wore shirts with Mickey Mouse on her chest. We found that by tugging at her shirt, holding it a certain way, Mickey Mouse would smile. Or laugh, sometimes, even cry.

When I left for home every evening I would see her stare at me from inside the living room, her tiny hands pressed to the bars of the window that opened to the street, her face screwed up with what I think were tears. Maybe as soon as I turned the bend at the end of the lane, she rushed straight back into her parents' arms, I don't know. Maybe she never thought about me when I was gone. But when I reached home it took me at least fifteen minutes to settle down, to put her away from my mind before sliding into my familiar world of dinner plates crashing against the wall.

'What was Sir's wife like?' he asks.

'She was sweet but she never really talked to me,' she says.

'What did she do when Sir and you were studying?'
'I don't know.'

I forget the exact sequence of events that night but what I remember is the voice of a woman crying. It was winter since the fan was still, I could see cobwebs across its blades, my little brother asleep by my side, a blanket covering us both. It must have been very late since I couldn't hear anything from the street outside, the pigeons in the cage must have been asleep. The last trams and the buses must have gone, I could only hear the chiming of the clock in the living room. And a woman crying.

I climbed down the bed, rubbed off some of the sleep from my eyes, stood behind the drapes, looked into the living room.

Sir is talking to my father, who has one hand on his shoulder. Sir's wife is standing in one corner, trembling. I can hear her cry like a baby. On the table, in the centre of the room, is a small white bundle, smelling of Dettol.

I walk closer to the bundle, no one asks me to stop, no one seems to have noticed that I have entered the room because no one asks me to go back to my bed and go to sleep.

The baby's eyes are half open, her hair wet, her face white as if someone has sprinkled an entire can of Cinthol powder. Her tiny arms stick out of the pink towel that drapes her body, one on each side, her fingers are curled. She's wearing a frock I have seen: a blue frock with Mickey Mouse smiling on her chest, its ear pressed against her heart.

She is dead.

'How did she die?' he asks.

'I don't know. I heard later that she was in the hospital for a few days, some virus had entered her brain.'

'Are you sure?'

'I don't know.'

Sir picks up the bundle, lifts the arms and tucks them in.

'You want to come?' he asks me.

No one protests, Sir's wife is still crying, although now silently. Father is now standing in the veranda smoking, looking at the empty street, the tram wires glinting in the dark.

I say yes.

There's a rickshaw waiting outside. We trundle down

lanes, past people fast asleep on the streets, a cow sniffing at a garbage heap, past the sweet shop with one shutter missing.

I want to ask what happened but I know it's too late, I can feel the baby's legs press against my elbows. Sir is staring into the night in front of him, above the rickshaw-wallah's shoulders.

We cross tram lines, shudder over cobbled roads, meet one broken Calcutta Milk Van tottering down the road. Sir's watch says 3 a.m. We smell the river from a distance, the sludge and the smoke. At this time, there aren't any funeral pyres burning, just a cloud of smoke from those that have burnt in the evening, this cloud mixing with the fog.

The man behind the counter is fast asleep. Sir knocks at the wooden board propped up outside, he wakes up, gives him a slip of paper to sign something on and then calls out loud. A boy pops up from the shadows, like a ghost, leads Sir to the steps of the ghat.

'Get her,' he says. And the rickshaw-wallah hands me the bundle; the baby's head rests against my chest, she isn't heavy but still my arms hurt as I hold her, dead, a cold wind blowing the smoke into my eyes.

'Come with me to the steps,' Sir says, and he takes the bundle from my arms. The boy leading us, we walk down, there's a dirty moon in the sky. The river is one big black table top glistening in the dark.

Far away, I can see the steamers bound for Gangasagar, their lanterns flickering. The wind tears the fog and the smoke in patches through which I can make out the dark shapes of the Howrah Bridge.

Sir walks into the river until the water reaches his chest, he lets the baby go, there's a splash, the ripples reach my feet, drench my slippers. And she is gone, sucked in by the Hooghly.

We wake the rickshaw-wallah, the journey back home begins. Nothing has changed, we pass the same people sleeping on the same pavements, past the same cow sniffing at the garbage, past the sweet shop with one shutter missing.

At home, Father is ready with a bucket of steaming water. You have to take a bath, he says.

Sir and his wife leave. And at around four in the morning, with an albino cockroach staring at me from the drain in the bathroom, I am naked and wet, my periods have begun, my tears mix with the water and the grime, I can smell the smoke in my hair, I can see the water, mixed with the soap, my blood, glide past the white cockroach. Into the city's drains that pump themselves into the river where the baby lies fast asleep.

'How do you remember all this?' he asks. 'The cockroach, the water in the bathroom, after so many years?'

He can feel her shiver, he puts his arm around her, he can feel the warmth of her breath, the softness of her body, they snuggle close.

'I saw it first on the night of our wedding. And then several nights.'

'What did you see?'

'I saw the dead baby.'

'What do you mean, you saw the dead baby?'

No, not the dead baby. But its footprints. It must have been around three or four in the morning, you were fast asleep since I lifted your arm, placed it on the pillow, switched on the lights and went to the bathroom, and despite all this you didn't move even an inch.

The bathroom was dry and just as I stepped in I switched on the light and there they were. Tiny footprints on the red tiles. At first, I didn't even notice, I just switched on the light and then went to the blue bucket. When I bent down to fill the mug, I saw it.

Footprints on the tiles, four little dots of water and a tiny patch, the imprint of a tiny foot. The prints were in pairs as if a baby had dipped its feet in water and walked all around the bathroom. I could count about a dozen of them.

I still didn't know what to make of these until I saw the albino cockroach. It hung, upside down, from the wall. Exactly where the cockroach was that night when I stood naked, watching the water and the soap glide across the floor.

Suddenly, everything came rushing back to me, Sir, the baby girl, the rickshaw ride to the burning ghat, the cow and the garbage heap, the river and the ripples, the baby's dead arms pressing against my elbow.

And I stood in the bathroom for quite a while, frightened, not knowing what to do, whether to scream or to wake you up. Should I pour the water over my feet, pour more water until the footprints dissolved? I thought for a while and then washed my feet with mugs and mugs of water. It flowed all over the floor, across the red tiles and within a minute the entire floor was wet, the footprints had gone.

I got up again, it must have been about an hour later because the floor was dry, the water had dried. Except for the footprints. They were there again, this time in different places.

The same footprints, four to five little dots of water ringed around a little patch. It was as if the baby had come in my absence, dipped its feet into the water and walked all over the floor again.

I wanted to wake you up but through the window I could see the morning light, a dull grey stain had already appeared in the sky and it made me feel better. Maybe it's memory trying to swim to the surface, I don't know. I covered my head with the blanket and went to sleep.

It was there again the next night, yesterday night. The same footprints, the same cockroach. Why has the baby come back to me after all these years? How do these footprints appear? Is the baby still alive?

'Please help me,' she says.

'Tell me what happened to the baby,' he says.

'She died. I just stood there, on the steps, watched it sink in the river.'

'What happened before she died?'

'What do you mean?'

'Think,' he says. 'Think hard, think about those stories you told her, the games you played with her dress. What did he do to you when you were sitting in front of him?'

'Who did what to me?'
'The teacher? What did Sir do?'
'I don't remember anything,' she says.

She is fast asleep when he gets up and walks to the bathroom, the red tiles are dry, he takes a jar out of his pocket, releases the albino cockroach near the drain. The cockroach first flutters for a while, its wings blur and then they come to rest as it hangs, upside down, from the wall in the drain.

He balls his hands into two fists, dips them in water and then he goes down on his knees, crawls on all four, along the tiles, printing tiny feet on the bathroom floor. Then he dips his fingers in the water and prints the toes.

It's very cold and he shivers, his back hurts, his body supported on his hands, his knees press hard against the tiles, he is careful so that water doesn't spill.

It takes about fifteen minutes and then he gets up, switches the lights off.

Maybe she'll remember more and more, he thinks, keep diving into the depths of her memory, through the highwayman and the old inn door, below the ghostly galleon tossed upon cloudy seas until she comes to what Sir did to her so that he can wipe her slate clean, rub everything off so that they can go into the future leaving her past behind.

But it doesn't happen that way at all, it can't happen that way, he will not be able to wipe her slate clean. He will try hard, he will dot the bathroom floor every night but one night she will discover and run away. Your mother, my sister.

Second-Last Story

⟶⟫⟨⟵

The pen now rests on the paper, its job done, its nib catches the light from the table lamp but it doesn't glint as it should. That's because it isn't so dark now, there's other light coming into the room, the first light of the sun, through the green window, its wooden slats, through the red curtains.

It's a weak light, part blue, part white, the yellow will take at least an hour, but it's a persistent light. Envious of the table lamp, it pushes itself into the dark corners of my study, under my table, behind the book-shelves, in the space between the door and the wall.

And then it begins to silently dry, one by one, the black pools of shadows which have gathered during the night.

I have to get up.

The chair makes a noise, my feet rub the floor, I can hear one sparrow, it must be the one with the black bib which keeps hopping all around my balcony during the day.

The fridge still coughs, the tap in the bathroom has stopped dripping. They must have switched off the water supply sometime during the night while you were sleeping and I was pulling the words out of the air in my room. Lining them up on my pages, like schoolboys and schoolgirls waiting for a drill. Telling them to march, left, right, left, right, about turn, attention, stand at ease, telling them to dismiss.

Now they are tired, each page sleeps covered by the other. There's just one thing left before I am done. I have to search for the lampshade.

For that thirty-year-old lampshade made of cane lying in the storeroom, next to the kitchen, along with other things: the mallet Bhabani used to clean the clothes with, the red bicycle Sister got from Grandfather, the black coat Father got on his wedding day, the red socks I wore when snow first fell from the sky.

Once I find the lampshade, I shall clean the cobwebs caught in between its slats, carefully, so that baby spiders don't get hurt. I shall wipe the dust and then I will bring it to you, my child, and put the shade on the lamp, switch it on, but wait.

*

Wait.

Before all this, before all that, I need to put your mind to rest, no one's going to take you away. I shall call up Mr Chatterjee, tell him that he doesn't need to wait any more, the man and the woman will surely find another child somewhere in this city of twelve million, a child at some hospital, unclaimed and unnamed, one they can call their own. If not today, they will get the child tomorrow. Or the day after.

So it shall be I who will take you to the Alipore Zoo, to the Birla Planetarium. We shall watch baby monkeys and mother monkeys, the tiny torchlight, shaped like an arrow, that flashes, darts across the huge black hemispherical dome. We shall find out where Jupiter is, try to understand why we have evening and why we have night, I will tell you all the stories that didn't make it this night.

As of now, however, let me get the lampshade and switch it on.

So that the light falls in a million specks on the blue bedspread making our sky shimmer with stars. And let me lean over you and spin the shade so that the stars move in orbits across the bed, over your body, your fingers, across the two pillows, which serve as your walls, in the hollows where my fingers were.

I am tired, I shall quietly remove one pillow and lie down beside you, adjust myself so that your head fits exactly in the curve of my neck. Let us sleep for a while because tonight is the night they will all be there, we shall wake up only when the stadium is full, the microphone is ready, the amplifiers have been tested. For tonight is the Eden Gardens night.

EIGHT WORDS

He's standing in the centre of Eden Gardens on top of a towering stage, more than one hundred feet high, draped with white silk, ninety-five thousand people sitting around him, waiting for him to speak.

It's an evening, December, cool, a wind blowing from across the river has dried the city, brought light shawls, sleeveless sweaters out. They have painted the stands at the stadium, the cricket season begins in two weeks. They have switched the floodlights on and so high is the stage that when he looks down he can see their bright haze as if it's morning, stained by smoke from some fires lit somewhere near the stadium.

Above him are the stars in the sky, as faint and as high as they were from his bedroom window. To his left is the Howrah Bridge, he can see the winking lights of the steamers, the clock tower at the railway station.

The air is unusually clear tonight for he can see beyond that, much beyond that, over the railway platforms, the sheds, he can see a train coming in, a passenger train, its yellow windows like a string of lights being dragged along by a child.

He can even see the dark forms of a man and a woman, perhaps husband and wife, standing at the entrance to one of the coaches in the train.

No one's talking. Down below, he can see their faces, all ninety-five thousand, turned towards him. He can make out each face distinctly, old and young, even babies, women with saris across their shoulders, men on their way home from the office, their leather suitcases on their laps. He can see a child turn to his mother, she lowers her face to kiss him on the forehead, a man near her lights a cigarette.

He can see the potato chips boy, the blue and orange plastic packets between his fingers. There are some faces he can recognize. There's a man, drunk and laughing; a woman standing near a white washbasin in one corner of the stands. There's a man in glasses waving at her; a woman from Sarajevo, her red scarf; an old man, bent from his waist, painting glue onto aluminium cans, a woman in an oversized nightgown talking to her nurse, both smiling.

*

There's a beautiful woman in a blue sari and a sleeveless blouse, her arms as white as milk. She's holding a picture book with drawings brightly coloured on paper that shines.

The microphone stares at him, like an injured puppy he's picked up from the streets, its eyes closed, its snout turned upwards, waiting to be petted. He can see its steel frame, the semicircular black base that strangles its neck.

He clears his throat, there's a hush as the noise is magnified what seems like one thousand times. The microphone whines.

The doctor, the one with arms as white as milk, smiles at him, he can see her lips move, she's telling him to write it down.

'Write it down,' she's saying, moving her lips, hoping he will lip-read.

But it's too late, everything is set, they are all waiting.

So he goes up to the microphone, taps it once, taps it twice, he can hear the wind in his ears, the first nervous coughs from the crowd, the first fidgets, someone gets up to walk out, he clears his throat one last time, and they all look at him as he begins to whisper the words he's been waiting to whisper.

And because he cannot say the sentence all at one time, because the doctor, the one with arms as white as milk, has made him recall that afternoon when he lay on the carpet, the words growing and growing until they filled his lungs, he breaks up the sentence, one or two words at a time so that he can take long breaths in between, give each word the air it needs to travel across the city and ninety-five thousand people.

So the first word he says is *I*, it floats all around the stadium, brushes against the faces of the people he knows, the strangers he has seen who look at him, through the haze, the second is *am*, his lips open and close, he can hear his breath through his nose, a hiss in the microphone, like a wind blowing, and they are all now waiting for the third which is *the* and no one notices, it's a common word, an article, used and reused in almost every sentence they hear, and so it flutters for a while and then silently flies off into the sky but it's the fourth word, *father*, when some faces light up, some faces darken, he can see someone gesture towards him, there is a roar in one corner of the stadium, someone's shouting something he doesn't hear, he can see an old man standing, gone is the fat around his waist, he goes on to the next word which is *of*, and he says it pretty fast because it's a word that's neither here nor there, what does it mean, no one knows, and he needs to end the sentence now since it's already getting very late and he can see some people getting up, preparing to leave, he has to keep them back for that extra second or so because they need to hear it all, that's what he has been waiting for, the whole night, and he says *my* and they stop, some turn back, it's beginning to get personal, a sudden interest surges through the crowd, he can see Bhabani standing in the crowd, clapping, she looks at him as he looks at the microphone again, the puppy seems fast asleep.

Through the corner of his eye, over the heads of the ninety-five thousand people, he can see the railway tracks coming in from the darkness, glinting in the light of the giant halogen lamps they have put up at the station to prevent thieves from ransacking the store or even ripping off the fish-plates and selling them as scrap at the Howrah foundry market, it's time now for the last two words, *sister's* and *child*, there, it's done, the eight words have been spoken, they have flown, each word across the city, like eight pigeons in flight, in the night, white against black, he doesn't have to lie any more, twist facts to flesh out his fiction, he coughs once to clear his throat, coughs twice, and then he looks down to see the belt in his trousers firm and stiff, he breathes in hard, the tummy doesn't droop, he adjusts his shirt, walks down the steps that lead off the stage, they are all standing now, some clapping but he doesn't hear because he has to be home in time for his daughter to wake up, to open her eyes.

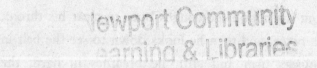